P G SPENCER

Chocks Away!

To Kate

Enjoy!

Written as a challenge from a very close friend (you know who you are, Sarah!), this is dedicated to a young lady called Annabelle, who is now custodian of Casey.

In addition, I'd like to recognise my writing mentor and friend, Sarah Mackie, for support, encouragement and practical guidance, and also my children and long-suffering partner who, I am sure, would prefer to remain anonomous. Thank you!

If animals dream like us, where do they go in their slumber?

Jason G Goldman

Chapter 1

Thwack!!!

The blow to his back caught Casey completely by surprise, and sent him spinning into the hedgerow. He lay there, stunned for a moment, not having any idea what had just happened.

Breathlessly, he popped his head out of the undergrowth, to check if the coast were clear. Seeing it was, he crawled out from where he'd landed, turning around to face the direction of whatever caused the blow. Had it been a predator? Maybe a fallen tree branch? Or had he been caught unawares by his mortal enemy, Whistle, the farmer's guard dog?

Up to that moment, the early morning had been pretty much like every other morning. Perhaps a little boring, though we all do like our routine, don't we? Today, typically, Casey woke up at 5am thinking of eggs. It was an early March morning, so the dark of night was starting to turn into a misty early dawn. Casey likes this time of day. It's still quiet, and he can forage for food without worrying too much about Farmer Wuxter or his big black and white border collie dog . A nice quiet start to the day, when he can forage and daydream.

You see, Casey has dreams, he has ambitions. He...

But wait, you haven't met Casey yet! Let's put that right, let's give him a wave and say "Hello".

Oh, you can't see him? Oh dear, Casey is very shy. He doesn't like to be seen by people, he much prefers to hide amongst the woodland trees and grass. He is there, though. Say "Hello Casey" and look very closely in the picture. You may just spot him.

Look out for a large tail and pointy ears. Casey's fur is orange, with a white tummy and black legs. He has pointed ears, with long nose and whiskers. Oh yes, you see, Casey is a fox.

Casey loves the great outdoors and his local woods and forests, but always dreamed of travelling. He wanted to explore the world, foraging amongst the trees and exploring new places. When he's up high up in the trees, watching everything around him, he daydreams of adventure, exploring new places, and searching for things that he loves. Like food!

Casey loves food. He's especially fond of peanuts, fruit and cheese. He does like to hunt, and sometimes will catch a rabbit, or maybe a bird or worm. In the wood, though, Casey really likes berries and fruit. He picks them when they are fresh and ripe, and eats them for breakfast.

Well, foxes don't really think of eating breakfasts – they just eat when they are hungry. But, when Casey gets up in the morning at first light, the berries and fruit are easy pickings, still covered in dew and a delicious start to the day. So we could say that he likes berries and fruit for breakfast! And eggs - which is what Casey was thinking about when:

Thwack!

Casey had been peering out of the undergrowth for several minutes, and could see nothing in the immediate vicinity that could have attacked him. Only then, though, he spotted the airport perimeter fence and noticed that, stuck against it and protruding through it a little was a black square object on wheels. He'd been standing against that fence, looking for a curlew nest, and the square thing must have caught him when it hit the fence. Casey's territory is very near an airport, and it seemed that a small suitcase had spun off the trolley as it was heading towards an aeroplane ready to be loaded onboard. The suitcase was on wheels, and it had landed on the airport tarmac with a thud, then, before anyone noticed it had come loose, it had taken off and disappeared, bouncing along into the fence. When it hit the fence, it caught Casey on his back, propelling him to the ground.

Casey climbed out of the hedgerow, and examined this black square object. He found, quite quickly, that, by digging a hole underneath the perimeter fence, he could touch the object. So

3

he did touch it. No reaction. Then he prodded it. Still no reaction. Then he caught hold of it with both paws and found he could drag it under the fence. In doing so, the small suitcase opened, spilling its contents of clothes all around him.

Casey had never seen anything like this before. The case was easily large enough to accommodate him, and it was nicely padded. He soon found that he could make himself very comfortable, very comfortable indeed, by snuggling up in the suitcase among the clothes.

Already, the morning was turning into something a little different from the normal, and Casey found this exciting. Somehow, he figured this new toy would become very important to him and would help him realise his dream of exploration, adventure and travel. By now, though, he was getting hungry and it was becoming fully light. Casey started to feel a little worried that Whistle the border collie dog or Farmer Wuxter might be out on their morning rounds. So off he scuttled, stopping by the nest of a curlew on the edge of Farmer Wuxter's field to take one of her eggs for breakfast. Then Casey made a mental note to investigate this new toy more, as he headed off to the safety of his burrow until later.

* * *

Whistle and Casey had history. Of course, all foxes are wild animals, and they forage and hunt small animals, birds and eggs. Farmers don't like foxes, as they often steal the eggs from the chickens, and one of Whistle's jobs on the farm was to protect the chickens and their eggs from those pesky foxes.

One day, when Casey was much younger, Whistle caught Casey in the act of taking eggs from one of the chicken coops. A long chase ensued, with Casey snaking to the right, then the left, into the undergrowth and deep into the trees in his attempt to escape. Not to be outdone, Whistle, older but wiser, was able to anticipate Casey's moves and almost managed to trap the little fox against a tall oak tree. Almost, but not quite, as Casey, in an instant, darted up high into the tree, higher than Whistle could climb.

Whistle could still see Casey there, sitting in the tree, enjoying that egg he'd stolen from Whistle's chickens. And as he watched Casey consume that egg, he swore the cheeky fox actually winked!

Since that day, Whistle has lost no opportunity to catch that naughty fox. Though Casey was by no means the only fox in the woods, it was Casey that Whistle paid particular attention to on his daily round with the farmer. One day, he'll make a mistake. One day, one day.

Whistle was pulling harder on his lead and making that excitable sound that old Farmer Wuxter recognised. He's caught the scent of a predator! The farmer deftly slipped the lead of the dog, and off he went, into the undergrowth, sniffing, sniffing, sniffing.

Casey! That cheeky fox had been there, and very recently. He sniffed and sniffed, following the trail of scent that Casey had left that morning. He followed it to the airport perimeter fence. He followed it into a patch of undergrowth that had been strangely flattened, as if something large and heavy had dropped onto it. He followed it down a narrow pathway into the trees. Suddenly, it disappeared. Whistle stopped, paused, looked all around. Despite sniffing almost every blade of grass, Casey's scent had been lost. It seemed that, once again, that pesky fox had outsmarted the old dog. Frustrated, Whistle made his way back to Farmer Wuxter, nuzzled into his leg and waited for the farmer to look in his pocket for a biscuit. "One day", thought Whistle, "I will catch you, Casey".

* * *

Foxes make their homes by digging burrows in the ground called "dens" or "earths". Their burrow gives them a cool area to sleep, a good place to store food and somewhere safe to have their pups. Lying deep in his burrow, Casey had heard the commotion above him at ground level, and quietly smiled to himself (foxes can smile). He waited a little while silently in his burrow, then, when the sounds and smells of the farmer's dog disappeared, he completed his breakfast with a few mouthfuls of the berries he'd foraged earlier that morning. Then, after a huge yawn, he was asleep.

* * *

Casey's nap was filled with thoughts of eggs, berries, barking dogs and a suitcase. As he dreamt, he found himself hiding in the suitcase, safe and sound, as the demon dog sniffed around, unable to get at him. Somehow, Casey found he could see out from inside the case, but of course, Whistle the dog could not see in. Then, as his dream continued, he found himself on an adventure, travelling the world inside this magic suitcase, far away from Farmer Wuxter and his dog.

New, exciting places, adventures and experiences, they all appeared to Casey in his dream. And hawthorn shoots. His dream was suddenly full of the scent of hawthorn shoots. And that's when Casey woke up, yawning again, and feeling rather hungry. Luckily, he'd stored some tasty hawthorn shoots in his burrow, peppery and very buttery, and he settled down to eating those, wishing he still had the egg from that morning, and thinking about his dream and that suitcase.

Once he'd finished eating, he popped his head above ground, carefully, in case Whistle was around, and sniffed the air. No sign of danger, so out from the burrow he clambered and made towards where he'd quickly hidden the case earlier. It was still there, untouched, still with the clothes spilling out from the opened case.

Carefully, Casey climbed in the case once again to have an even closer look. He was surprised by how soft the inside of the suitcase was. The lining was deep and padded, and amazingly comfortable, much more comfortable than his burrow. He found that he could lift the lid and close it while still curled up inside. And so, after a while, Casey decided that the suitcase was rather warmer than his burrow, had plenty of space to keep food warm and dry, and, if he did one day find a mate and have children, it would be safe for them too.

Over the next few days, Casey developed a new routine. He still sneaked around the chicken coop after eggs, he still looked out for Whistle, the farm dog, he still climbed trees and foraged in the woods. But also, Casey spent time every day playing with his new toy, the suitcase, and wondering if, one day, that dream of excitement and adventure could come true for him. After a while, Casey found that if he burrowed his little fox body into the clothes, he'd be even cosier. He found he was spending more

8

time curled up in the suitcase that in his own burrow. Then one day, he abandoned his burrow completely and made the suitcase his new home.

* * *

One morning, not long after, while looking through the airport perimeter fence, he started noticing what people wear as they got onto their aeroplanes, noticing the pieces of paper and little red books they carried. These seemed to be important in some way, as they always had to show them to the person at the door of the aeroplane. Casey had no idea why these pieces of paper were important, but then, one day, while fiddling with the zip on the suitcase, he was surprised to find pieces of paper fall out that were just like those that the passengers were using!

The little red book had a picture of a man. He had ginger hair and a little beard and wore glasses. Now Casey had found a pair of glasses just like the one in the picture hidden in the suitcase, so he managed to put them on. With the glasses on, everything became blurred, so he took them off again. However, this did interest Casey, and (he's a clever boy) he wondered what he look like with them on. Being a clever boy, Casey knew that if he looked down into the local pond, he could see a reflection of himself, so off he scuttled to the pond. He popped the glasses back on, and looked down into the water...

What he saw surprised him so much, he let out a little yelp. Foxes can make yelping sounds. In fact, they can make 28 different sounds when they want to. Casey hasn't counted then, though: foxes can't count (or maybe they can, but just choose not to tell). And just then, Casey wanted to yelp! Because what he saw was himself, wearing the glasses, and not looking so very different from the picture of the ginger man he'd found in the little red book!

Chapter 2

Foxes are active throughout the year and do not hibernate. They're mainly nocturnal, and often they are active mainly around dusk and dawn. Typically, foxes spend the day resting in cover.

Casey isn't a typical fox! He rests through the day, but he does this by finding a nice shady spot downwind, so that Whistle the dog can't sense his scent. As long as he's out of sight and can't be sniffed out by the dog, he's safe and can relax and think.

Casey is a red fox – very common around the world, and some say quite an attractive variety of fox. Like most red foxes, Casey has a bushy orange tail with a white tip, known as the tail's tag. Foxes use their tails to signal to other foxes, as a form of communication. They can also signal other family members that prey is near. They don't generally look very much like people, though, even ginger-haired bearded people wearing spectacles.

After he tried wearing the spectacles, Casey did a lot of thinking. Then he did some more thinking.

His favourite cover for the days was facing the airport buildings. From there, he could see all the people lining up to board the planes, and knew that, somehow, the pieces of paper and little red books were very important. Now Casey is a clever boy, and had worked out that the pictures of the people in the little red books probably needed to match the faces of the people boarding the planes. See how clever he is!

So this morning, as the sun began to warm the day, Casey did some more thinking. Then he did some more.

Then he suddenly had an idea.

The thing is, with the glasses on, Casey thought he looked a little bit like the picture of the ginger-haired person with the beard that was in the little red book. But he also realised that he didn't look enough like the picture in the little red book.

But Casey had an idea!

Casey (he IS a clever boy!) had noticed that all the people getting on and off the planes recently were all dressed up, and had coloured masks over their faces. That meant that the little pictures in the red books wouldn't match completely to the half-hidden faces of the people getting on the planes. So, he thought, if Casey could find something he could use as a mask, then maybe, just maybe, he could pass for the picture of the person in his little red book. How cool would that be?

So Casey started making his plan...

* * *

From the departure gate, a line of people pressed towards the open doors of the aeroplane. All were wearing masks, and these masks had a variety of patterns and colours. Some people actually coordinated their masks with the other clothes they were wearing.

It was a warm morning at the airport, and as the people lined up to enter the aeroplane, the sun sparkled on the sunglasses many were wearing. With those, and the masks, it was quite difficult to see much of their faces.

One by one, they carried their small bags up the stairs, then, as they got to the doorway, they showed someone their boarding pass and passport, before pressing into the cabin to find their seats.

While the passengers queued, other activity was happening around the belly of the aeroplane. People in dark uniforms and high visibility jackets were loading large suitcases from a trolley train, into an open hatch. There seemed to be a never-ending pile of these cases in lots of different patterns, colours and designs. Finally, though, the activity seemed to be complete, and the hatch door in the aeroplane was shut tightly. The high viz jacket people climbed back into the trolley train and it snaked off away from the aeroplane.

Another team of high viz people poured out of a large lorry, shaped like a huge tube. From the lorry, they pulled a long thick hosepipe from the back of the tube, and carried this to the underside of one of the aeroplane wings, before attaching it somehow to the wing. They left it there for a while, with one of the high viz people fiddling with levers at the back of the lorry tube, until, seemingly satisfied, they pulled the pipe back to the lorry and coiled it safely in its cradle.

Soon, and one by one, the jet engines started up. First with a low whine, then rising to a deafening roar, the engines came alive, creating a reverberation that went right through the plane. The aeroplane was getting ready to fly!

Soon, the plane was moving back from the gate, until there was enough room for it to turn around so it was facing outward. From there, it started off toward the take-off runway, gathering speed until it was travelling at the speed of a galloping horse.

Arriving at the take-off runway, the aeroplane stopped for

a moment, then the engines rose to a crescendo of noise, and suddenly, the plane was moving! Faster and faster along the runway it went, until suddenly, it started to leave the ground. The nose of the aeroplane started to point up towards the sky, and the aeroplane was airborne.

Within a minute, the plane had climbed high into the sky, higher than most birds, and then it turned away. For a moment, the plane seems to be poised in the sky, with a full view of the underneath of the wings, then it was gone, flying off into the distance.

All of these activities had, on this morning, been closely scrutinised from the wood the other side of the airport fence. Casey had been making mental notes of everything he saw, and building it all into a plan that, he hoped, would get him onto a real aeroplane. He just needed to refine this plan a little more, so throughout the day, he watched, as each plane came into the airport, discharged its passengers and cargo, then loaded up again for another flight. And each time he saw this, his plan became more detailed.

* * *

Foxes tend not to travel by plane.

There's probably a very good reason for that, but, if there is, Casey hadn't heard it. More than anything, he wanted to be inside an aeroplane, feel it rolling down the runway and lifting into the air. He watched others travelling this way for so many days. He'd come up with a plan, he'd refined it and now, he felt his plan was fool-proof.

Part of his plan involved timing. He knew that it would be difficult for him to pass easily for the person in the picture in the little book he had found, even with the dark glasses and mask on. So very early in the day, just before first light, might be a good time to make his attempt. And 5a.m. is one of Casey's favourite times of day, and great for foraging. It's early enough not to be worried by Whistle the dog or Farmer Wuxter, and 5a.m. by one happy coincidence, is when Casey knows the early morning aeroplane is getting ready to fly.

Now Casey had no idea where the flight was heading. Casey doesn't know geography, doesn't understand countries or different types of woodland. Or maybe he does, but chooses not to tell us. He's only ever lived in Boxer Wood, so that's all he's aware of. No matter, he decided, once and for all, to make a break for it.

So, by 5a.m. this morning, Casey had his case by his side, mask over his nose, glasses over his eyes, ready to attempt boarding the plane. First, though, he needed to find a way through the fence to get to the plane. Hmmmm, perhaps he should have

15

thought of that earlier. Fail to plan, plan to fail, or rather, fail to plane!

Quickly, Casey scanned the bottom of the fence, in both directions as far as he could see from where he stood. There did seem to be a weak spot, where the fence didn't quite meet the ground, a little way away. Dragging the suitcase, Casey quickly scuttled across to that part of the fence. This was the point where the suitcase had originally landed, but could Casey himself squeeze through?

Now foxes tend not to travel by plane, but they do tend to be very good at squeezing through fences. Casey is particularly good at squeezing through fences, which may be why Farmer Wuxter and Whistle the dog always seem to be chasing him. It's a simple misunderstanding, of course, Casey just doesn't realise that the chicken eggs in the chicken hutch aren't ALL meant for his breakfast!

The problem here, though, wasn't just about Casey squeezing under the airport fence. No, it was about Casey squeezing under the airport fence with a suitcase. "Think", he thought...

First, Casey scrambled and dug a little gap under the fence, making that gap bigger and easier to get through. Then he scrambled through it. Next he reached back through the fence to grab the suitcase and... Couldn't quite reach it.

By now, it was getting lighter, and already, Casey could hear sounds on the airport runway, where people in high-viz jackets were coming and going about their business, getting the plane ready to take off. "Hurry", Casey thought...

Scrambling back into the wood, Casey pushed the suitcase so it was very close to the fence, then performed a comical fox-limbo under the gap in the fence, then reached back for the suitcase. He stretched and stretched his fore-paw until he couldn't stretch any more and finally felt the leather of the handle, grabbed it and dragged it under the fence onto the runway. "Good", he thought, "I'm in!"

Standing close to the fence with the suitcase, Casey was still a distance away from the aeroplane. He could see it clearly, though, standing proud on the runway, with the morning sun reflecting off the body of the craft and a gentle throb of energy around it. "Could I really make it onto that plane?" thought Casey?

He'd been over the plan a thousand times. Climb the stairs once almost all the other people had boarded, make sure mask and glasses are hiding his face as much as possible, and hold up the all-important pieces of paper in front of his face to hide his own face even more. There, what could possibly go wrong! And wait, just then, in front of him, he saw a line of people walking solemnly towards the plane, ready to board.

"It's now or never" thought Casey. Using first the long grass at the end of the runway as cover, then the buildings and vehicles as he got closer to the plane, Casey was able to join the end of the queue of people snaking towards the aeroplane steps without being noticed. His heart was racing, his eyes darted from right to left to see if anyone had noticed, his ears pricked up to listen out for any sounds that suggested danger. "So far, so good", he thought. And suddenly, he was at the bottom of the steps.

This was it, his chance to fly at last. All he had to do was climb the steps, slip in un-noticed and he'd be away! Just to the top of the steps...

Half-way up the steps, a sudden roaring noise startled Casey. To his right side was one of the huge engines of the aeroplane. Of course, Casey doesn't know much about engines, and he certainly doesn't know anything about the Trent 7000 Engine sitting in its nacelle under the wing. Over 3 metres wide, slung underneath each wing of the A330 Airbus that Casey was in the process of boarding. All Casey know was it made a sudden roaring sound, and that frightened Casey so much he let out a "yelp".

Now foxes can make around 28 different sounds though they are a mostly silent. You are most likely to hear one of two distinctive fox noises, and for a male fox like Casey, the usual one is like a loud 'A-woo!' that sounds much like a domestic dog. When Casey heard the engine roar just inches from him, the sound he made was not one of the 28 sounds that foxes make, it was a new sound of terror. "YELP".

Casey stopped dead in his tracks. Had his squeal attracted any attention? His eyes scanned around and up to the top of the steps. The last few people were boarding the aeroplane, squeezing past the two people in friendly blue uniforms who smiled as everyone passed them. His ears fully pricked up, checking for sounds of commotion. Nothing (whew). The roaring noise had probably drowned out Casey's yelp. "Keep going", thought Casey, "Don't give up now, you're nearly there".

Onwards he climbed, one step after another, and then he was nearly there. So very nearly there. On the last step, when he heard one of the friendly uniforms let out a very unfriendly scream.

Looking up, he caught the start of a huge commotion in the doorway, as the two uniformed people started what looked to Casey like a little dance, but what actually was the cabin crew jumping up and down in fear of a fox at the top of the aeroplane steps. "Shoo" they started to shout, and very quickly indeed, Casey realised that his plan to fly needed a re-think. Better to withdraw than be caught.

Foxes tend not to use stairs. Luckily, though, they do tend to climb trees, so Casey was able to turn on his back paws and run straight down the steps and across the airport runway, before the uniforms had a chance to "Shoo" again! Casey found the gap under the fence, pushed the suitcase through in front of him and quickly joined it, on the Boxer Wood side, before escaping deep into the wood.

The early morning activity had really tired Casey out, and normally by this time, he'd be snoozing anyway. Not today, though. Through yawns and occasional pawfulls of hawthorn shoots, he went through the morning, step by step, to unearth what went wrong and how his plan needed to change so he could, at last, travel on that aeroplane.

There had to be a way. There had to. A yawn turned into a stretch, and another yawn, and Casey drifted off into a sleep full of roaring engines, aeroplane steps and uniforms shouting "Shoo". And while he slept, a new plan formed in his dreams.

Chapter 3

Human beings dream most nights. Sometimes they'll remember their dreams the next morning, sometimes they won't. Some people dream in colour, some people dream in black and white.

Do you have a cat or a dog, dear reader? If you do, it may often look like they are dreaming when their whiskers twitch and legs wiggle. Does your pet do that? I'm sure it does.

But do animals really dream like human beings? Since you can't observe another creature's dreams directly, there's really no way to know for sure if it's dreaming. But over many years, scientists have found some pretty convincing, though indirect, evidence that many other mammals and birds do indeed dream.

Casey dreams, and though he doesn't realise it, Casey has programmed his unconscious mind with the problem of how to board an aeroplane safely and fly to somewhere new. We do that sometimes as well: if we have a problem, or something we are wanting to do, we'll write notes, lists, and diagrams about the problem we want to solve.

I'm sure you'll do the same: you'll read books, watch YouTube clips and talk to other people who might help. You'll cram all that together, in your head, and by doing that, you'll point your subconscious mind towards the solution. Then your unconscious mind suddenly wakes you up with the perfect solution! You'll notice this has happened sometimes when suddenly, the name of that pop group you couldn't remember yesterday pops into your mind, or the perfect answer to a difficult situation that happened a few hours ago presents itself to you.

Casey didn't know any of this, of course. Casey is a fox! However, when he woke up the next morning around 5a.m., to the sounds of the birds singing and the early flight powering up its engines, he knew EXACTLY what he needed to do to get aboard that plane.

The previous day, Casey had been watching aeroplanes get ready for flight. As usual, passengers were lining up to climb stairs. As usual, some people were leaving cases at the bottom of the stairs, for the high viz people to load into the cargo hold.

This day, though, was different. A young well-dressed couple were travelling, and though Casey had no idea who they were or where they were going, he did notice their suitcases.

These were not ordinary suitcases: they were magical! Obediently, they followed the young travellers a short distance behind them, as they marched to the front of the line of waiting passengers. They didn't drag the cases behind them, they didn't

22

hold on to the handles, they just walked, and the cases rolled along behind them.

This, to Casey, was pure magic. To human beings, though, they are called smart robot luggage that can follow you automatically. A famous writer, Arthur C. Clarke, once said "Magic is just science that we don't understand yet" and for a young fox who has never heard of smart robot luggage, nor Arthur C. Clarke, for that matter, this was indeed true.

Casey was fascinated by what he saw. Suitcases that rolled along by themselves! And the strange thing was, none of the people seemed to notice.

He thought and thought about this amazing sight all day, until the sun started to hang low in the sky, and the sunny day turned cooler. Casey curled himself into a tight little ball, to keep himself warm, and went to sleep, still thinking about the magical suitcases that move by themselves.

This was how Casey primed his unconscious mind, to use what he had seen, and everything else he had experienced, to come up with a solution to the problem of him getting on an aeroplane without attracting attention. And this is why, when Casey woke up the next morning at 5a.m., to the sounds of the birds singing and the early flight powering up its engines, he knew EXACTLY what he needed to do to get aboard that plane.

* * *

One thing was clear to Casey – he needed to do a little preparation, and also some simple testing. So he started with that, as soon as he'd woken up and found some tasty treats to eat.

First, Casey tried some young hawthorn shoots. By early March, hawthorn is one of the first trees to really wake up after winter so that's the perfect time for picking the fresh young leaves before they toughen up and become unpalatable. In the past the leaf and unopened flower buds were a favourite forage for children, known as bread and butter – the leaf being the bread and the flower the butter.

Next, he found some goosegrass: this is an easy one to find and abundant and is really starting to shoot up by March. It's known by most people as the plant you pick to throw on your friend's back as it sticks to clothes, but Casey likes it when it's young and tender and good to eat.

Finally, he found a big clump of dandelion – every part of a dandelion is edible for humans as well, and again, Casey enjoys a few mouthfuls while planning the day.

Finally, Casey managed a huge yawn and stretch, then off he went to get his suitcase.

The first test was a simple one: Casey stood up the suitcase so it was standing on its four wheels, then slowly walked away from it. Was the case starting to follow him? Sadly, no.

Next, he tried to call the case, using the "wow wow wow"

sound that some people mistake for a bird song. The suitcase didn't move.

Casey then tried a whistle, but unfortunately, foxes cannot whistle. Instead, Casey tried a number of high yips and yaps and other assorted calls from his repertoire of 28. The suitcase stubbornly refused to move.

By now, it was becoming very clear to Casey that his suitcase was not a magic one after all. He'd tried everything, but nothing he tried made the case move on its own.

Some foxes would have given up by now, but Casey isn't just any fox – he's a very clever fox indeed. So if he couldn't get the suitcase to move on its own, could he make it move if he climbed inside it?

A moment later, he had scrambled inside the suitcase and found that, by moving around inside it, the case did roll a little. The problem was, though, he couldn't quite control the direction of travel, and the case often just went round in circles or bumped into trees.

On a normal day, by now, Casey would have been curled up in a tree having a snooze, making sure he was well away from Farmer Wuxter and Whistle the dog. Today, though, he was so absorbed by trying to get his suitcase to move where he wanted it to move that he'd totally forgotten to feel drowsy. Suddenly, though, a breeze passed him by on which was the unmistakable scent of Whistle. The farmer was on patrol!

In a flash, Casey hid the suitcase behind a bush, covering it with twigs and leaves to make sure it was completely covered. He then picked up a fallen tree branch with his paws and carefully removed all the traces of his morning's activities in the ground, by brushing the branch around the woodland floor. Satisfied that he'd hidden his shenanigans effectively, he climbed deep into a hole in a rotten tree that was close-by. He took one last look around to make sure that there was nothing around to indicate his recent presence, he snuck deep down into the tree hole, and waited, the hair on his back and tail standing up, as does when a fox feels under threat.

Whistle wasn't a bad dog, as such. He helped the farmer look after the farm by guarding it from intruders. He helped the farmer by rounding up his sheep. He loved Farmer Wuxter, because the old man looked after him and was his constant companion. Well-disciplined, faithful, dependable and devoted, he was always protective towards the farmer, his family and the farm. In fact, to the farmer and his family, Whistle was a very good dog and loved as one of the family. To Casey, though, and any other woodland predator that ventured onto Farmer Wuxter's land, Whistle was a mortal enemy and a risk. In particular of course, one of Whistle's duties was protecting the farmyard chickens, so when Casey, or one of his brethren, managed to get into the chicken coop to steal their eggs, Whistle would be very upset and would spend the rest of the day sniffing around looking for the culprit. If Whistle found the fox that was stealing those eggs, it would be bad for the fox. Very bad...

A moment after Casey had hidden in the tree, the farmer rounded the corner, with Whistle the dog straining on the lead. He had caught the scent of a fox! Although Casey had squeezed himself deep into the hole in a tree, he could hear the sounds of the old farmer wheezing with the effort of holding his dog back, and the sound of the dog sniffing hard around the bushes and trees. Minute after minute passed, and the sounds of the activities around Casey's hiding place got louder and louder. If he looked into the hole in that tree, Casey would be finished!

The little fox had curled himself into as tiny a ball as possible, to give himself a little protection, and now he lay perfectly still, trying to make even his breath as quiet as possible.

Minutes passed, and it seemed to Casey that Whistle would never stop searching around that tree until he found him, and because of where he was, he'd have no means of escape. The dog's sniffing got louder and more persistent, and Casey had to stifle a whimper of fright. Then, Casey heard the old farmer talking, and suddenly heard the "twang" of Whistle's lead as the farmer pulled him onwards to look elsewhere. Footsteps got quieter and quieter until they were out of range even for Casey, and at last he felt he could breathe.

Casey lay still in the hole in the tree for a long time, just to make sure the coast was clear. By then, it was nearly dusk, and Casey knew that the farmer and his dog would be back at the farm house, eating their dinner, so he knew it would be safe for him to venture out again. He looked towards the farm to check that all was clear, then acted.

With light beginning to fail, Casey once more examined the suitcase. There must be a way he can direct where it goes while he is inside the case...

Casey hadn't noticed this before, or if he had, he hadn't given it any attention. Whilst the suitcase was made out of a very hard material that Casey couldn't break if he tried, the middle section, where the two halves of the case met, were made out of a woven fabric. This meant that, depending on how much stuff was placed in the case, it could expand somewhat to fit everything in.

That middle section, then, could be ideal for Casey, as with a little gnawing, he could easily make a hole in the bottom of the case so he could fit a leg through and guide the suitcase, making sure it got to the aeroplane.

With only a few moments of good light left, Casey got to work. The hole would have to be on the bottom of the case, where the wheels were, so that when he pushed his leg through, his paw would be able to touch the ground. Casey pulled, gnawed and nibbled along the bottom woven piece of the case until suddenly he found he'd made a small hole. It needed to be small so that he, and the other contents didn't fall out. But it needed to be just big enough for him to squeeze his little leg through.

Excited, he clambered back into the suitcase, closed it with a click, then pushed and pushed his hind leg at the tiny hole until he felt it slip through and touch the ground. With no time to lose, he pressed his paw to the ground and push. He felt the suitcase move, and each time he pushed with his paw, it moved further and a little quicker. Until it hit that old dead tree with a thud!

Ah! Direction... That's something he'd have to think about again. But with daylight nearly gone, Casey decided that an answer for that would have to wait until the morning. And he knew just who would be able to help him!

Chapter 4

Foxes live on every continent except Antarctica. They can thrive in cities, towns and, of course, the country. But despite being all around us, they're a bit of a mystery to many people. So, for the curious:

Foxes are related to wolves, jackals and dogs but unlike those relatives, foxes are not pack animals. When raising their young, they live in small families, or "skulks", in underground earths. Otherwise, they hunt and sleep alone. Casey had left his burrow last year along with his five siblings, and that was not long before he found his special suitcase that he now uses as his safe place to sleep.

Now it's not that foxes don't have any friends at all. Foxes are known to be friendly and curious. They play among themselves, as well as with other animals, like cats and dogs do. They love balls, which they often steal from back yards and golf courses.

They usually prefer life on their own, though, and because they are true predators, hunting small birds or mammals and domesticated animals such as chickens. As a result, they have few friends in the woods, though Casey, being a particularly friendly young fox, had become pals with Spike, a local hedgehog Though they didn't see each other every day, they knew where to find each other for playtime, and, towards the end of March,

Spike's hibernation was over.

So straight after breakfast the next morning, Casey made his way towards Spike's den. As the name suggests, hedgehogs are often found near hedgerows – they "hog" the hedges! These are places for hedgehog nests, providing a good supply of food, protection from predators and safety of movement.

Farmer Wuxter's pastures are also ideal foraging areas for hedgehogs like Spike, so it was no surprise that Spike lived in a hedge, on the edge of the wood and alongside the old farmer's cattle pasture. And that's exactly where Casey found him that morning.

Casey and Spike enjoyed playing together with balls that Casey had found in people's gardens. They quickly learned, though, that the bigger balls often went "pop" when one of Spike's spines stuck in them, so they found that smaller, harder balls were better, and lasted longer. Spike kept one hidden in his hedgerow, and immediately dragged it out as he saw Casey approach.

Casey gave his gekkering sound, that foxes make when play-fighting as cubs or playing later in life, and they spent ten minutes whooping together playing with the ball.

Spike was worn out quicker, and when he dropped back from the playtime, Casey did the same and they sat together for a few moments gathering their breath and sharing their news. Casey bemoaned his most recent run-ins with Whistle the dog, and how he had bravely avoided Whistle the day before. Spike wanted to know more. Spike hadn't had the same experience of Whistle, and saw him in a very different light. Attentive, clever, conscientious, faithful and altogether virtuous, to Spike, Whistle appeared a very good caretaker of the farm.

"Well", started Casey, "he's on my tail every day, he seems

31

to think that every egg that disappears from the chicken coop is taken by me, and that's not the case!" Spike replied "I do understand how you feel, but do you understand how Whistle might feel when, every day, he sees you taking another egg from the chickens?"

"Well yes, I suppose," accepted Casey, "but I'm not greedy, I only take the one, and the chickens always lay an extra one, I think".

Spike was a wise old hedgehog. He prompted Casey for a deeper conversation about what he thought might be important to Whistle, so that maybe Casey would understand him a little better. "Well, he likes discipline, things to be in order in the farm, everything in its place, everything spick and span. I've even heard the farmer's wife say that! He's very protective, but too aggressive and doesn't tolerate me being anywhere on the farm".

"I see", continued Spike, "so think about yourself for a moment, what is important to you?" "Well", said Spike, "that's easy, it's..."

"Go on", Spike prompted, "do you like predictability or doing stuff in the moment? Do you like discipline or high-spirits?" Casey thought for a few moments. It wasn't easy for him to put these things into words. Finally, he ventured "I suppose I love the idea of adventure, exploring new things, I'm a bit of a dreamer, but curious, resourceful and playful. And I do have a huge imagination!"

"Exactly", said Spike, "so the things important to you are very different from the things that Whistle values. And to add to your list, which I do agree with, you are adventurous, bold, clever and resourceful, but you are also quite impatient."

Casey looked a little sheepish but had to agree with Spike.

Spike summarised "So is there anything wrong with being adventurous and resourceful, or for that matter, disciplined and ordered?" "Well no", admitted Casey, "they are just different". "Exactly", said Spike triumphantly, "so maybe if you respected what was important to Whistle, he may be a little more tolerant to you. Just try being a little less mischievous and annoying to him, you'll see!"

Casey was starting to find the conversation a little difficult, so moved on to the reason for his visit.

Casey told Spike about the suitcase, about his dream to find adventure and excitement, and fly on the aeroplane. He told Spike about the attempt he'd made pretending to be a passenger, and the narrow escape he'd had. He told him about the new idea he had, and how he'd made it possible to move the suitcase while hidden inside it. Then he asked Spike for his help.

Casey needed to be able to see where he was going from inside the case, and to do that, he needed one or two eye-holes in the side of the suitcase. Now Casey's dexterity in hole-making was good enough for making big, untidy holes, but not anything smaller or more neat. The question, then, was "could Spike gnaw spy-holes in the suitcase so that Casey could see the direction in which he was travelling?"

"Hmmm, interesting", thought Spike. He was keen to help, and had a reasonable idea of what Casey needed. To be sure, though, he'd need a proper look. So they immediately set off the short distance to where Casey had hidden the suitcase.

Of course, foxes are swift little creatures and can move very quickly when they need to. Hedgehogs have surprisingly long legs too, around 10cm in length. These are usually hidden under a hedgehog's spines, and are only really visible when they are running. This means that hedgehogs can run a lot faster than we might expect of them, and on this day, Spike was able, just about, to keep up with Casey as he led the way back to his hide.

Slightly out of breath by now, Spike immediately assessed what was needed and got straight to work. Now hedgehogs have five-toed, clawed feet enabling them to run, dig and climb, so Spike started by trying to work a clawed toe into the weaving on the side of the suitcase. That proved impossible, so he tried nibbling away at the fabric to try and start a hole. A few nibbles later and success! A tiny hole appeared in the fabric, and Spike was able to work his toe into it and stretch it gently so it became the size of a small spy-hole.

Casey was super excited, and couldn't wait to try it out. Into the suitcase he scrambled and found that, with his leg poking through the bottom of the case and adjusting the direction of the case, he could use the spy-hole to see where he was going. Perfect! In fact, so perfect that he didn't think he'd need a second spy-hole, so Spike's work was complete.

By now, it was nearly time for the old farmer's morning round, and because of that, it was time for the two friends to make way back to the safety of their homes in the wood. Casey thanked Spike for his help and promised he'd be over to see him again for playtime very soon. Time, then, for a few stretches, a big yawn, and settle in for a day of dreaming.

* * *

The following day, a late March Sunday morning, the clocks had gone forward an hour during the night. As a result, it was still quite dark at 4:30am, when one of the refuelling crew began to prepare the aeroplane for its new load of aviation fuel. The first, and most important job, was to bond the aircraft to the refuelling vehicle before connecting the refuelling hose - bonding prevents any spark when the ground operator connects the refuelling hose to the aircraft coupling. The cable on the A330 Airbus connects to a fitting on a main landing gear undercarriage.

All done and made safe, the fuelling began and around 20 minutes later, the aeroplane was ready, the bonding cable disconnected and the fuel truck on its way to its next job.

Meanwhile, of course, there was much more activity around the plane. A ground power unit was towed out by a squat "tug" to supply power to the aircraft, another truck brought the flight's supply of refreshments for its morning journeys and, of course, the baggage conveyor cart- the one where an inclined conveyor belt brings in luggage ready to load into the cargo bay.

Except the baggage conveyor cart was still inside the departure building, as one of the high-viz crew had forgotten the change in time and hadn't adjusted his alarm clock! Tomasz, his friend and co-worker, was calling him urgently to get him in, so that the flight could leave on time, and, the call made, Tomasz started working as fast as he could to load up the baggage on the baggage trucks.

Meanwhile, inside the Departure lounge, the flight had been called to the departure gate, and as it was the first flight of the day, it was going to be a busy one. In ones and twos, with occasional larger groups, the passengers snaked back in a line from the departure gate at the terminal, with their carry-on luggage gathered around them, and boarding cards and passports at the ready. Shrill announcements from time to time, bounced around the departure hall, advising that early boarders would be called first, followed by families with children and those passengers needing special assistance. Once these groups had boarded, the remaining passengers would be called.

Another message warned that some baggage would be held back from boarding as "carry-on" due to limited cabin space. Those bags would have to be left at the bottom of the passenger boarding steps along with any prams and pushchairs. As this was a small airport and didn't have airstairs for passenger boarding, specially-designed trucks delivered the passenger steps to the aircraft for boarding and disembarking.

By the time Tomasz's work partner, Bogdan, had arrived, most of the passengers were already on board the plane, and settling down into their seats. Together, they marked off the last of the passenger bags, then raced out to the plane as fast as the conveyor cart would go, and as it was still quite dark, they failed to notice one bag spin off the conveyor as they took a tight corner to approach the aeroplane. The errant bag flew off into the undergrowth, bouncing along and becoming completely hidden from view.

Arriving at the aeroplane, Tomasz and Bogdan quickly loaded the baggage into the cargo hold, then made their way to the passenger steps to pick the bags that had been set aside to make room in the cabin. Tomasz made a quick count of 4 pushchairs and 14 bags, and between the two handlers, they popped the bags into the cargo hold and quickly as they could. Finally, they checked against the baggage manifest. Hmm, it appeared there was a slight mistake on the manifest, though on a physical count, the number of bags did seem to add up. So, off they went and cleared the area, taking the baggage truck back to the departure building ready for the next flight. It was going to be a busy day!

In the cargo hold, all was quiet, including inside one particular bag that had appeared quite unnoticed, at the bottom of the passenger steps, helped that morning by the additional cover of darkness. Casey had hardly dared breathe, in case someone heard him, even as the case was lifted and thrown into the cargo hold. Casey was well-protected with the collection of clothes that was still inside the case, so he'd been able to cosy himself up into a nice tight little ball, and he was no worse for the manhandling. His was a mixture of excitement and trepidation, and the realisation that at last, he had made his plan come to life and he was about to go somewhere – where, he has no idea – on the adventure of his life!

The next second, Casey was shaken by a deafening shrill, prolonged whine that nearly made him cry out loud.

Chapter 5

On board the aeroplane, a young married couple, Maisie and Tim, were settling into seats 23F and G. Not ideal for them, as the two seats were split by an aisle. However, it was close to the mid-cabin toilets and the mid-cabin galley, and further by the fact that there was no row of seats directly behind them (so no possibility of being disturbed by a naughty boy kicking the back of their seat!)

Maisie and Tim had met 14 years ago when stationed at a holiday rep apartment on Ibiza's Playa d'en Bossa resort. Fresh-faced and just out of college, they loved the lifestyle of being holiday reps, and when love blossomed and they got together, they decided to make their careers in tourism. So now Maisie was a Health and Safety representative, making sure that the travel company's hotels and excursions were safe for their clients, and Tim looked after customer satisfaction, which meant checking that the service given in their resorts was of the right high standard. They had travelled around the world in these roles, and even today, 14 years after they met, they looked forward to any opportunity to travel.

Of course, they could have elected to sit next to each other, however, a little lady by the name of Elina was installed in 23H, the window seat. At 9 years of age, she could see out of the window without straining her neck, and had been watching the activities outside the aeroplane since settling down into her seat. A curious young lady, determined, quite tall for her age, with short mid-brown locks and a full, round face, Elina often preferred to play with boys, and liked nothing better than to run around in the local parks near where they lived, climbing trees and creating mini-adventures.

Elina was the product of Maisie and Tim's happy marriage. Elina was also quite a seasoned traveller for her age, and if she had any questions or concerns, she knew that her mom and pa had all the answers. In particular, when a small child, Elina had been quite a nervous flyer, and often worried about those strange aeroplane sounds. Over time, either Maisie or Tim had put her mind at rest and she'd learned to listen out for and anticipate those sounds. In fact, she'd learned what sounds different aircraft make. As they were on the Airbus A330, Elina knew to expect a "thump" when the main landing gear struts extend to their full travel on take-off, and three short beeps from the direction of the cockpit just before final approach to landing, (the warning that autopilot has been turned off). She'd also expect a "barking" noise when the Power Transfer Unit (PTU) would activate during taxi in and, of course, one of the first noticeable sounds before take-off, the loud "poof" as the ventilation switches from an outside system to one inside the aircraft. Later, when airborne, Elina would listen out for the whirring sound as the flaps first increase the wingspan and then retract to help give lift, so the plane can take off and maintain air speed, and towards the end of the flight, the "Bang" From the belly of the plane, heard on descent at around 2,000 feet when a flap under the wing opens and the landing gear drops. Understanding what the sounds mean had given Elina confidence and now she found those sounds reassuring, and part of the thrill of flying.

As she watched the goings on outside, Elina asked "Mom, what's that long whining noise I can hear now?" Maise smiled. She knew that noise signified that loading of the plane was just about complete and they'd be on their way soon. "Elina dear, that's just the electric hydraulic pump used to open and close the cargo doors. You'll hear it again the other end of the flight when the ground crew unload all the cases". Elina smiled back, and turned back to the window, feeling both excited at the upcoming flight and tired from the early morning start.

Just then, the lights in the cabin flickered briefly, and the sounds of the air circulation system stopped, just for a second. Again, Elina looked up at her mom, the tired smile showing the slightest frown of concern. "Don't worry about that, angel", Maisie reassured her daughter, "the lights will always flicker as they swap from the ground power generator, to the plane's auxiliary power unit. The APU powers an electric generator that powers the electrical system on the aircraft when the main engines are off and provides pneumatic pressure for air conditioning and, more importantly, starting the main engines. They often put the power across to a ground unit when holding on the stand, as it's cheaper to power the plane that way, and saves burning fuel while on the ground. Now relax, we'll be leaving very soon and we'll be on our way. So let's all check we are properly belted in!"

Elina didn't have long to wait. A sudden jolt signalled that the manoeuvring tug had started to push the aeroplane back of its stand. In tandem with this, Elina heard the mighty Rolls Royce Trent 700 engines as they came to life. Her father smiled across the aisle: "Chocks away!", he exclaimed. Elina knew what that

41

meant: a chock was a wooden triangular block of wood that, when placed under the tyre of a jet, stopped any involuntary movement on its stand. "Chocks away!" was called by the pilots to indicate that they were ready to take-off. The ground crew would then remove the chocks in front of the aircraft's wheels, ready for take-off.

The sound of the turbines built as the tug continued to move the aircraft back of its stand, until it stopped, its work done, and the ground crew disconnected the towbar, freeing the aircraft in readiness for its taxing manoeuvres towards the runway.

In another moment, the engines had built up to a steady roar, and Elina once again felt a slight jolt, this time in a forward direction, and the aeroplane started on its winding way towards the runway. During that time, the cabin crew introduced themselves and presented their safety demonstration. Although Elina knew these well from previous flights, she also knew it's always wise to listen out for these. So over the next 5 minutes, she learned how many rest rooms and exits were on board, where the life vests were stored, how the cabin lighting worked and, should they be necessary, from where the oxygen masks were deployed.

The timing of the presentation seemed perfect. As soon as the cabin crew had finished, a curt "Cabin crew, prepare for take-off" message came across the tannoy, and the crew took their seats, buckling up just as the plane pivoted to point directly at the end of the runway.

There was a pause, then the passengers heard the noise of the huge engines build to a mighty crescendo. Elina held her mother's hand and squeezed. Then the captain released the brakes, and the aeroplane began to accelerate down the runway.

Faster and faster it went, and Elina started to hear "ker-clunk, ker-clunk" sounds coming from the aircraft tyres on the tarmac, changing from "ker-clunk, ker-clunk" to "kerclunkkerclunk clunkclunk" and then, suddenly, the front wheels of the plane lifted and the jet began it's climb into the morning sky.

* * *

Hidden within the suitcase, and with old clothes wrapped around him for comfort, Casey couldn't see much from his spy-hole. He could see the outline of other suitcases around him, but in the dim lighting, he couldn't make out anything more.

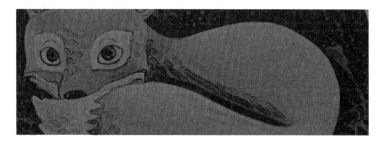

The shrill whining had stopped, thank goodness, and in stop-ping, it appeared to have cut out most of the light. This meant that Casey's ability to spot anything more than shadows was very limited indeed.

The noises though. Every sound he heard was frightening. Noisy, mechanical, amplified by the cargo hold and scary. Casey's little heart raced and, for a moment, he wondered if he had been silly in his attempt to fly away on this aeroplane.

The hair stood up on his back and tail, which happened whenever Casey felt threatened.

It was too late now, though, and Casey felt the jolts of movement, as the aircraft first was pushed back from its stand by the tug, then as it made its taxi journey to the runway. At last it stopped. "Whew" thought Casey, "I'm glad that's over".

All of a sudden, though, the engine roar rose to a scream and the aircraft started to move again. Bumpity bump, as cases moved around and Casey's suitcase slid down into a pile of other cases. Bumpity bump, as the plane continued to accelerate. Bumpity bump, the tyres of the aeroplane thudded against the concrete runway. Bumpitybumpitybumpitybumpitybumpitybu mpitybumpityumpumpump. Then, without warning, Casey felt something strange in the pit of his stomach, as if everything he'd eaten that morning suddenly weighed more than it had before. Then he felt the whole world tip over, and he fell backwards in the case. He rolled himself into the smallest little ball he could and closed his eyes tightly. He let out a little whimper.

Dear reader, do you find yourself being startled by a sudden noise, or a sudden movement? Do you also find that, even if there's a loud noise around you, if it's a continuous noise, it gradually becomes less noticeable? Well, perhaps you have a few things in common with foxes!

Once the aeroplane had finished its initial climb and levelled out, the roar of the engines became a continuous throb. Though very frightened indeed, the little fox found the sound of the engines gradually sending him to sleep, helped by two things, one being that it was now mid morning when foxes often have a long snooze, and by the fact it was getting cold – very cold.

Once the flight reached cruising altitude of 38,000 feet, the outside temperature would become minus 45 degrees Celsius. Now that's very cold indeed. A person would not survive in that temperature, but then again, a person wouldn't be able to roll into a furry ball inside a suitcase full of old clothes.

Casey was able to snooze for much of the flight, woken from time to time when the aeroplane needed to make route changes. When that happened, sometimes the aeroplane would roll over to one side or the other and the engine note would change. Casey would stir, worry for a few moments then drift back to sleep. In fact, the aeroplane was crossing the Atlantic, south of Iceland and then flying down the east coast of the United States, but of course, Casey had no knowledge of this, because he was totally isolated in his suitcase cocoon and had no concept of the passing of time.

Once, Casey was woken, startled, to the aeroplane shaking and bobbing about. It felt as if his whole tummy was being lifted up to his throat then dashed down into his boots! Of course, the little fox didn't like that sensation at all, and rolled himself into a ball even tighter than before, closing his eyes as tightly as he could to make the feeling go away. The swashing and shaking only lasted a few moments, and within a few more, the drone of the engines had sent him into another sleep.

That sleep was finally broken by a strange popping sensation in his ears, and another change to the sound of the engine. He found himself needing a big stretch and strained his little muscles to make himself his full length – difficult to do in his confinement. New noises started to join the note of the engine, first a whirring sound that started and stopped several times, then a bang and shudder that made Casey jump. The aeroplane felt as if it was slowing down, as Casey's weight seemed to be shifting in the suitcase, and after a few more minutes there was a loud bump, a few bounces and a very loud screech and Casey found himself thrown to one side of the suitcase. Then, after another moment, the bumping and bouncing became a more orderly feeling of movement, and somehow, Casey knew instinctively he was back on the ground. But where?

* * *

Up in the cabin, in seat 23H, Elina had enjoyed breakfast, then a movie, then some computer games she enjoyed playing, then a snooze. In common with a certain little fox, she had also been disturbed a few times by course corrections, and in particular, a little momentary turbulence over the Atlantic. She'd also woken fully for a surprisingly tasty lunch, with an apple pie dessert, her favourite.

Finally, after another movie, she felt the aeroplane making its initial descent. A loud "ping" accompanied the seatbelt sign, and this was reinforced by a tannoy message from the cabin crew to put the seat backs up to the upright position, put seat belts on, lock the tray tables and open the window blinds. Elina yawned and stretched, and waited for some familiar sounds: First a whirring noise as the flaps increased the wingspan of the aircraft to aid stability as it started to slow down. Then, at around 2,000 feet, a loud bang, as a flap under the wing opened and the landing gear dropped. Elina knew these sounds and knew they were quite normal, and was ready when the aeroplane made its final touchdown to the squealing of its brakes, as it slowed quickly from its landing speed of nearly 150 miles as hour to a stop just before the end of the runway.

Many fellow passengers gave the crew a round of applause as the aeroplane touched down, and then, after a few moments of taxiing, the aircraft made its final stop on its stand at the airport arrivals terminal.

"Welcome to José Martí International airport", said the captain over the tannoy, "we hope you've had a pleasant flight and enjoy your time here in beautiful Havana. The time is now 11am, so we are 5 hours behind UK time - remember to set your watches folks, and enjoy amazing Cuba!"

Chapter 6

Dear reader, have you ever ridden on the most scary fairground or theme park ride you could imagine, been thoroughly terrified while on it, then immediately wanted another go when it finished?

Well, that's exactly what Casey **didn't** feel! He had had enough of flying, and couldn't imagine being trapped in the cargo hold of an aeroplane ever again. He just wanted to get away into the undergrowth as quickly as possible and recover his thoughts. And he was hungry!

Like other omnivores, foxes are clever at stockpiling food. If they come across a large supply of food, they will store anything they don't eat right away to feed on later. That's exactly what Casey had done before the flight, and around the old clothes in his suitcase, he'd packed berries and nuts for the journey, not knowing exactly how long that journey would take. That supply had nearly run out though, and Casey was starting to wonder what he'd be able to find to eat in this strange new place.

Those thoughts were interrupted suddenly by the shrill, pro-longed whine heard of the electric hydraulic pump used to open the cargo doors, and within a minute, he was hearing the sounds of people moving around in the cargo hold placing the cargo of cases onto the conveyor of the towing truck that would carry them to the arrivals conveyors. Then suddenly, he felt his case, with him still inside, being roughly picked and tossed onto the conveyor, where it snaked down onto the bed of the truck. Soon, he felt the motor of the towing truck start up and he was again on the move. Apart from the movement, the surprise for Casey was the difference in the smell of the air around him. It was suddenly very warm indeed, dry and with a heavy sweet smell, unlike anything Casey had sensed before.

* * *

Elina and her parents were still sitting in the aeroplane awaiting the buses that would take them into the arrivals terminal. Elina could see the hi-viz workforce around the aircraft, like flies around a barbecue sausage, and the luggage tender arrival to start unloading the cases. By then, Elina was starting to get impatient, but then, after what seemed like ages, they were given the news that the airstairs had arrived and passengers could at last disembark. Priority, of course, was to those 36 passengers sitting in the Business Class seats, and they all took the first bus to the terminal. Elina and family grabbed their carry-on bags and pressed down through the aisle to the front exit and the steps once the Business Class passengers had left, immediately feeling the warm, dry air of late morning in Havana, The second bus was already nearly full and they felt lucky to just squeeze onto it before the doors shut and it moved swiftly around the terminal area, coming to a stop at a set of automatic doors.

Maisie and Tim had been in the travel business for a long time, but a few things about airports still puzzled them. One of those was the design. Did airport architects have competitions to find out who could make passengers walk the furthest to the aeroplanes or from them? It certainly felt like that in many airports, and this was one of them. Up an escalator, across what seemed like the whole length of the building, then down an escalator and another walk along the length of the building, before turning into the baggage collection area, which seemed to be immediately adjacent to the first set of automatic doors they'd entered the building through. One theory is that the "forced march" was timed to coincide with the time it would take the luggage to arrive on the arrival hall carousels, though today, after they had been through passport control and arrived at the carousel, this theory didn't seem to fit the reality that, as yet, not a single bag had appeared!

Some moments later, and a loud siren heralded the switching on of the carousel, after which bags started to appear. And this was another thing that, after all their years in the travel trade, still puzzled Maisie and Tim: if a family checks in three bags for a flight at the same time, and those bags are labelled and taken away together, why is it they never seem to appear the other end of the flight together? Today, this was certainly the case, and after 20 minutes of watching other people pick up their luggage and go, only Maisie and Tim had collected their bags – Elina's still hadn't appeared.

By now, only a few odd bags were on the carousel, and the very last of the passengers from Elina's flight were leaving the arrivals hall to look for their onward transport. The family was starting to feel concerned when, suddenly, a bag they thought they recognised popped onto the carousel. Recognisable yes, but looking a lot rougher than at the start of the trip. "Blimey", exclaimed Tim, "your bag looks like it's been pulled through a hedge, Ellie, I suspect we'll be needing to buy you a new one when we get home!" They were in a hurry after the long wait, so didn't spend too long examining the bag as they were conscious they had a taxi waiting for them outside. Examining the bag for damage would have to wait until they got to their resort, and they still had two hours of travel in front of them to get to their resort in Varadero. So Elina grabbed the handle of the suitcase and trundled it behind her as she followed her parents out of the airport, into the lunchtime sun and into the taxi.

Neither Casey nor Elina had any idea of the surprise that awaited them!

Chapter 7

The journey from Havana to Varadero is around 88 miles and takes around 2 hours. On this particular day though, in their taxi, Maisie had decided to do a quick tour of the Havana sights before heading to Varadero and their resort hotel. They passed through the vast Revolution Plaza, the site of many presidential addresses, featuring monuments to Cuban revolutionary heroes. They drove past the Museum of the Revolution, and Castillo De Los Tres Reyes Del Morro, a fort dating back to the 16th century and a symbol of Havana's seagoing past. Of course, they drove to the Plaza de la Catedral and the Old Town Square, and were heading towards the oldest plaza in Havana, the Plaza de Armas, when Elina started to question how long this journey was going to take. They had been up since 3am that morning, and by their body clocks, it would now be 7pm and nearly bed-time for Elina. Quickly, Maisie had a rethink and decided to make the straight dash to the resort. The grand tour could wait!

Their taxi, like many in Cuba, was a vintage American car of the 1950s and early 1960s. In their case, they were sitting in a 1955 Buick Roadmaster which originally would have been powered by a massive V8 engine. Like most of these vintage cars, though, the engine had long ago been replaced by Toyota diesel unit. So the car purred and jogged along, passing briefly through the beach areas of Plays Santa Maria del Mar and Playa de Jibacoa, then through Matanzas and the small town of Santa Marta, near where the Varadero Street market opens through the week selling handmade goods to the tourists. Finally, after a longer drive than any of Elina's family would have preferred, the taxi drew up to their entrance of their resort hotel.

Maisie's original plan around the quick tour of Havana city was partly to allow time for the paying guests who had been on their flight to get to the resort and check in. Her idea had been that, giving them that space, the queue to check in at the reception would be a little shorter by the time they arrived. In this, her plan had worked, and they were delighted to find there was no queue at all. Within moments, they had filled in the required forms, put on their coloured wrist bands and picked up the keys to their rooms.

The resort hotel was formed out of a main building, that house reception, a number of bars, restaurants and other facilities, then another block with indoor pool and fitness centre, then dotted around the main outdoor pools were the guest bedrooms, bungalows and suites. This was a substantial resort, and Tim had been given a small map of the area, with little red pen circles around the main reception and their own bungalow, which was facing the pool but set back far enough away not to be bothered by the noise of the children playing around it. They made the walk to their bungalow in just a few moments, with their cases dragging behind them. Tim waved his key card in front of the door lock and it clicked open. As they entered the bungalow, a wave of air-conditioned cool air wafted around them, which strangely had the effect of making them all feel immediately exhausted from their trip. However, a first look at their rooms was a must, no matter how tired they might be, so they went from room to room, admiring the furniture, the little touches like the vase of flowers and bowl of fruit in each of the two bedrooms and the overall space. Their bedrooms chosen (Maisie and Tim would, of course, have the big double room with the en-suite bathroom) they set their suitcases down ready to unpack and took stock. It was now 3:30pm local time, and they had missed lunch service, though none of them was particularly hungry at this point. Maybe better to have a snooze for a couple of hours, then decide what to have for dinner.

Elina had spotted the huge pool and, understandably, was excited and wanted an early dip. She was also very tired, though, and decided the dip could wait. Maisie and Tim were heading straight to their rooms, showering first then sleeping, and Elina agreed to do the same. Closing the door to her room with the decisive "click" that you only hear on hotel doors, she sat on the bed for a moment, deciding on what to do first.

"I know", she thought, "I'll pop my clothes into the wardrobe, then I'm unpacked and ready after my sleep". She stepped over to her suitcase, flipping it over on the floor and quickly unzipped it and pulled the lid back. What she saw made her eyes widen in astonishment. Clothes she didn't recognise at all were lying, filthy dirty, among what looked like brambles and crushed berries. Where were her clothes? Who did these belong to? Did something just move? What's.....?"

It wouldn't have been possible to decide on who screamed first, Elina or Casey! As Casey sleepily popped his head up out of a pair of gentleman's underpants, his eyes widened as they met the stare of a small girl inches away! It would also have been difficult to decide on who moved the quicker, Casey or Elina. Casey jumped out of the case in one leap, ran around the bedroom in circles and, in a second, had found a tiny gap between a cupboard and a wall, into which he squeezed himself, still squealing. Elina, however, nearly fell backwards as she jumped with fright, then launched up onto the bed, running on the spot with her arms flailing. If her parents hadn't been in the shower next door, they would surely have come running into the room to find out what the commotion was all about!

After a moment or two, Casey's energy for squealing had dropped somewhat, so he became almost silent (panting slightly) in his hideaway next to the cupboard. Elina's energy had also dropped and though she was still standing on the bed, she was motionless, and quiet, almost holding her breath, while she scanned the room. Their eyes met again, this time across the room, and this time, they both caught something of the other person in those eyes.

People say that the eyes are a "window to the soul" – that they can tell us much about a person just by gazing into them. Given that we cannot, for example, control the size of our pupils, we can sense much of a person's character, personality and emotion from their eyes.

For example, when we are excited or interested in what's going on, out pupils may become quite large. When less excited or interested, the pupils contract. So right then, both Casey's and Elina's pupils were biiiiiig!

Casey looked away for a moment. Animals generally don't like persistent eye contact, as it can make them feel threatened and defensive. Casey was, of course, trapped in the room with this young girl so did feel threatened a little, though something in that short eye contact with Elina made him think that the small child was a kind child by nature. Casey saw fright in her eyes but also a childlike curiosity. This was not a nasty person.

Elina also saw the vulnerability in the eyes of the little fox. She saw past his handsome little face into the soul of a small woodland animal that was not malevolent by nature and was, at this moment, frightened. That made her feel a little less scared of him, and in another moment, she had moved to a sitting position on her bed, trying to look as little a threat to the fox as she could.

Still in his hideaway, Casey relaxed a little, and adjusted his position so he was still ready to leap if needed, but could settle there if no threat to his safety. And that's where the little fox and young girl stayed for the next few moments, each getting used to being in the other's company.

Whether it was instinct on her behalf or simply her generous nature, but in the next moment, Elina had an idea. She needed to show the little fox that she was "friend" not "enemy", and an easy way to do that had presented itself in the bowl of fruit sitting on the bedside table. Picking up a large bunch of grapes, Elina, very gingerly, made her way across the bedroom floor, then held out her hand to offer the grapes to Casey. Casey stirred: he was, by now, very hungry indeed, and the grapes looked fresh and juicy. Perhaps if he were quick, he could take them from the girl's hand. So, summoning up all his courage, he took a small step out of his hiding place and gently dragged the grapes away from Elina's hand, immediately backing again into his safe place.

Within a moment, the grapes had been consumed, and Elina repeated the gesture, this time with an apple. That was accepted cautiously by the fox, and soon, the fruit bowl was emptying, as its contents were transferred via Elina to Casey.

Soon, Elina noticed that the fox was beginning to stock-pile fruit in the hideaway, and eventually, he pressed himself further back in his safe place and was out of sight. Elina, by now, had had enough excitement for one day, so with a wave of tired hitting her, she flopped onto the bed and was asleep before her head touched the pillow!

Chapter 8

"Ellie?"

"Ellie?"

"Elina?"

Elina woke to a very gentle prod from her mother. She opened her eyes to the sight of an unfamiliar ceiling, and for a moment, wondered where she was.

"Ellie, it's seven o'clock", said Maisie quietly, "time to get up".

Elina could see the light still streaming through the patio windows of her bedroom. Seven o'clock? Elina felt disoriented and wasn't sure if that meant breakfast time or evening. She may have slept round the clock, yet she still felt groggy.

"Ellie, it's been a really long day, I know, hunny, and we still have an hour or so before it gets dark. Do you want to have a quick look around the resort while we still have some light? Then we can go and get some dinner if you like."

Elina sat up and looked around. She suddenly started to remember the room, the suitcase, the fox...

THE FOX!!! She looked around again. No sign of the fox. Whew! Next, she processed her mom's question. Look around? Dinner? Eat? Yes, the mention of food suddenly made Elina wake up, and she swung her legs off the side of the bed and jumped down.

"Ellie, do you want a minute to change out of your travel things?" asked her mother.

Clothes, thought Elina, absent-mindedly. "CLOTHES"!!!!! Elina thought quickly. She had to tell her parents what she'd found when she opened her case. But the poor little fox – did she have to give him up? He looked so frightened, so loveable. Perhaps she'd save that part of the story for later.

Just then, her father breezed into her bedroom to join her mother. "Come on, Ellie, we're on holiday tonight" he said. "Phwoer, what's that funny smell in here, I'll get Housekeeping on that!"

Right, thought Elina, *it's now or never.*

"I think that smell isn't the room, it's the suitcase", she started. "When you two went to get showered earlier, I opened the case and found this", she said, pointing to the opened suitcase in the corner of the room. "Look, it's full of someone else's filthy clothes and rotten fruit. Somehow, I've got someone else's manky old case!"

Her parents quickly examined the suitcase. Sure, it looked identical to Elina's from the outside, but inside it was very clear that the contents belonged to someone else, and someone with very different hygiene standards! The case stank!

"Right", said Tim, "let's just get it out of the room for tonight. I'll find a place to dispose of it tomorrow, then we'll need to get you some new clothes, young lady, along with a new suitcase".

"OK", agreed Elina, and carefully picked up the old suitcase, opened the patio doors and placed the case on the terrace outside the room. She then closed the doors. "Ellie", suggested her mother, "why not leave them open a little, it'll freshen the air while we are out". "OK", replied Elina, reopening the door a few inches to let the cooling evening breeze into her bedroom.

"Come on then", her pa urged, "Let's see what this place is like and get some dinner, I'm starving!"

With that, the young girl and her parents made their way out into the early evening sun, for their look at the outdoor amenities they'd be using for the following week. The pool was enormous, and families were still having fun splashing around, even though, at this time of day, many had already made their way into the various restaurants for their dinner. As a result, the pool-side deckchairs and sunbeds were mostly free, and Tim (with his "travel company quality" head on) made a mental note to score these amenities well when he came to produce his report. For though they were at the resort as a family, the parents were both there to work as well, Maisie to ensure the facilities were safe and made the grade as a secure and healthy place for families to holiday, and Tim to made sure that visitors would enjoy their time there. As a result of this, they had already booked Elina into a number of day-care facilities, some including excursions, others including craft workshops, so she would not get bored and would be looked after while the parents were busy.

For now, though, it felt like a real holiday and the three made their way into a very nice looking restaurant to have their evening meal as the sun began to set over the spectacular ocean panorama beyond their resort complex.

Part of Elina continued to wonder what would become of that little fox, and indeed, what she'd find when she got back to her room.

Chapter 9

Elina had travelled a lot in her young life, and because of that, she was used to many types of cuisine. Cuban cuisine is mixture of Spanish, Afro-Caribbean, French & Haitian Creole and this first meal offered tastes of all these styles. Mixtures of tomatoes, lemons, peppers, seafood and spices accompanied by a variety of rice and bean sides weighed heavy on the restaurant buffet tables. Elina was hungry, but she was also tired, and rather than pick her way through these selections she went for the easy children's choice - burger and chips!

Maisie and Tim were more experimental, though didn't raise an eyebrow at what Elina brought back from the buffet. With plates full, they ate their food without comment, even a little mechanically, though everything had been prepared to perfection by the kitchen team. If you'd asked Elina's parents the next morning what they'd eaten, they wouldn't have been able to remember. In truth, the whole family was beyond tired, and needed their beds.

Between them, they decided to head straight back to the bungalow after the main course, though Elina did pick up an apple and small tub of ice-cream on the way past the dessert buffet, noting the typically Spanish influences of flan and Dulce de Leche among the ubiquitous pots of flavoured ice-cream.

Back at the bungalow, Elina quickly ate the small tub of ice-cream, then they quickly got ready for bed. Maisie and Tim gave warm hugs and kisses to Elina and made sure everything was locked up, then it was time for lights to go out.

Elina lay in bed for what seemed like hours, but was probably only a few minutes. The sound of movement from her parents' bedroom quietened, then stopped. Another few minutes, and still no sound came from the other bedroom, so Elina tip-toed out of her bed and quietly turned on her bedside light. She looked into the gap between that cupboard and the wall to see if the little fox was still there. No sign. She then quietly turned on the other lights in her bedroom, and explored the room, looking for any little space that a small animal could use as a safe hiding place. She looked under the bed: nothing. Under the chair: no, no sign. In fact, after a thorough examination of the whole room, it had become clear that the little fox was no longer in the room. It must have escaped, deduced Elina, while they were out and the patio doors were open.

Somehow, losing the little fox made Elina a little sad, but she guessed it would be a long way away now and she'd never find it. Pity.

By now, it was around 10pm in Cuba (so Elina had been up for a full 24 hours) and she was exhausted. Though a little sad at losing the fox, she was fast asleep within a moment, and she slept soundly and uninterrupted all night.

* * *

Casey had pressed himself back into the gap between the cupboard and the wall when the other people had entered the room earlier. The arrival of these people had frightened him a little more, and he didn't want to be discovered.

After a few moments, it seemed that the little girl was not going to give his position away, and indeed, the only thing that concerned him was his suitcase. The little girl was taking it out of the room. His case. His home! He hoped he'd be able to find it.

That opportunity soon presented itself, and one by one, the humans left the room, leaving the patio doors open to the outside world. Casey waited until all three had not only left the bedroom but also the bungalow, then very gingerly, he crept out from his hideaway and, whiskers twitching, poked his nose through the open patio doorway.

The smell of the air was intoxicating, filled with the fresh scents of herbs grown in the local gardens around the resort, often by local children. Oregano, chamomile, calendula and Japanese mint all combined to make the still evening air heavy and inviting for the small fox, and despite feeling very nervous, he could not resist creeping out on the terrace to take a look at this new environment.

The first thing he saw was his suitcase, Still lying open, as it had been left, this was at least one familiar thing to the small fox, and seeing it made him feel a little more secure and less afraid. So much so, that he was able to pluck up the courage to step off the terrace and explore.

What he saw around him was completely new and unfamiliar. Manicured lawns and flower beds, fruit trees, including the Caribbean guava, tropical flowers and palms. Casey had never seen anything like it. He explored further, keeping well hidden within the flower beds that were heavy with different coloured plants, then as he turned a corner and met the last glare of the sun, he suddenly became aware of crowds of people thrashing about in water. The last thing that Casey wanted was to be spotted by more people, so he quietly backed away into the formal gardens and continued his exploration of the garden landscape.

Foxes don't tell the time (or perhaps they do but just haven't told us), so Casey wouldn't have known it was 8:30pm Cuban time. He would, though, have noticed that it had suddenly gone dark, and though night-time is typically the time when foxes are most active, Casey felt this had been the longest day of his life and all he really wanted to do was find somewhere safe to sleep.

He retraced his steps until he found his terrace and suitcase, and within another moment, had curled up tightly into a ball amongst the familiar smells of the old clothes and fruit. He stirred once as he heard the patio door click shut sometime later, but otherwise slept through the night.

Chapter 10

Elina's family had slept soundly through the night, after a very long day of travelling. Although the sun had risen a little after 7:15a.m. it was a little past 8a.m. when Elina first stirred and gave a lazy stretch. Her mind felt a little detached and it took a few moments until thoughts in her head were beginning to focus. Holiday... Travelling... Swimming pools... Holiday... Fox...

FOX! Elina was out of bed, and examining all the small hideaway places in the room, to see if she'd missed the little animal last night. Nothing, no sign at all. Elina was slightly crestfallen, she'd rather hoped to see him again, it would have given her a fresh interest during the holiday.

Ah well, if he's gone, he's gone. She pulled back the curtains, slid open the patio door and peered out into the warm morning sun. Her eye caught that old suitcase, still lying open from where she'd put it last night. The pile of old clothes was still there, and as she looked, it stirred, as Casey tossed and turned in the case, wrapping himself even more snugly in the clothing. Elina smiled – perhaps she had found her holiday friend after all.

Just then, Casey opened his eyes and squinted into the day. His eyes caught Elina's look of friendship, and though still nervous, Casey somehow felt safe.

Elina was fully awake now, and realised she may only have

seconds to come up with a plan. Her parents were not up yet, but they could be at any moment, so priorities!

Elina was only 9, but she was very wise for her age. Her parents had taught her well, and she knew that panic always spelled danger. Her pa always cited his idol Arsène Wenger, the French football club manager, whose mantra was "Concentration, Calm, Control" – the three Cs. So now she concentrated – what key things did she need to do to protect the little fox? No panic, Calm: take it one step at a time. And Control: what did she need to control right now?

The priorities were very simple, Elina realised. The first priority would be protecting Casey from being discovered by anyone. Looking around her, Elina noticed there was a very mature garden all around the patio with excellent ground cover and tall bushes. Quickly, and without thinking of the little fox's reaction, she slammed the lid of the suitcase, and moved it into the undergrowth, so it was completely hidden from view. That done, Elina checked again from the patio – the suitcase was indeed hidden from view – she went back to it and gently opened the case. Casey's head popped out, looking slightly alarmed, whiskers twitching, but Elina's reassuring smile seemed to make him calm as well.

The second priority was food. Elina went back into her bedroom and found the apple she'd taken from the dinner buffet last night, and took that over to Casey. She guessed that would keep him going until the next part of her plan came to fruition.

Initial priorities covered, Elina relaxed, went back into her bedroom and had a wash.

* * *

Elina wouldn't have known, but during the night, Casey had been exploring. With the resort quiet and the guests asleep, it was a perfect opportunity for Casey to investigate his immediate surroundings and find safe passages. Safe passages would be runs he could escape into in a second, should he ever be threatened, and it would be important for the little fox to discover those early on, so that he would be prepared should the need arise.

That done, Casey surveyed the landscape. Heavy with bushes and plants, Casey was finding plants that he'd never seen before at home. Foxes are at home in areas which offer great shelter, so the overgrown gardens felt safe to Casey. The plants looked different, smelled different, and the insects living on them were different. But edible! Casey soon discovered the rich pickings in the undergrowth. Along with insects and crickets, there were berries and fruit to pick. Casey would not go hungry!

Suddenly, Casey realised he was not alone. He spied a small, rat-like creature out of the corner of his eye, and as he watched, he saw it was clawing bark off a tree and eating it – that must be his early breakfast! As it saw Casey, it zipped up a tall palm tree and disappeared. So, Casey thought, I do have company here...

Casey continued his exploration of the area, filled his tummy with the exotic mixture of fruits and berries, then, feeling a little tired, made his way back to the safety of his suitcase. A little later, he was woken by the stare of the small girl, who still looked more friend than foe. She presented him with an apple, which he hid away in his case for later, and worried him momentarily when she trapped him in the case for a moment. He soon realised that actually, she had made his environment much safer for him, as he and the suitcase were now hidden in the undergrowth outside the bungalow.

Casey felt relaxed. Maybe he had found a friend!

* * *

A little later, Elina's family were up, dressed and ready. They made their way to the breakfast buffet, and enjoyed a lovely variety of fruit, yoghurt, eggs and bread. Elina had taken a small plastic bag into the buffet, and made sure she loaded a few extra fruit and grapes into it to leave for the little fox later on.

As they ate, her parents planned the day. This was partly a holiday, and partly a working trip for her parents. Her father had appointments through the week, firstly to attend the resort's "Welcome" meeting, held for new arrivals throughout the season. That was 1p.m. in the main reception, so he'd be there straight after lunch. Elina's mom, however, had different priorities for the morning, and they involved replacing Elina's clothes and suitcase. Elina was, of course, still wearing her travelling clothes from the previous day, and was now feeling quite uncomfortable in them. Maisie planned to arrange a trip to the Varadero Street market, where she knew she'd be able to get all the holiday clothes Elina would need, and most likely a bag or suitcase for the return journey. Elina wanted to join in with the children's activities as soon as possible, but also wanted to be able to choose her own clothes, so she decided to go with her mother. As they'd be back for lunch, Tim decided to join them.

Arrangements made, the family quickly went back to their bungalow, grabbed what they needed, and made their way to the main reception. Before leaving the bungalow, though, Elina carefully placed her fruit cache next to the suitcase in its new undergrowth hiding place. Content with that, she joined her mother for the morning's adventure.

Chapter 11

Casey spent much of the day snoozing. The midday temperature had risen to 30C, which was so much warmer than the UK temperature of 6C the previous morning when his adventure had started. This warmth made Casey especially tired, and though foxes often catnap during the day, the weather in Cuba sapped his energy.

On the occasions during the day when Casey did stir, he'd yawn, stretch, roll around in the old clothes packed into the suitcase and fall asleep again.

On one occasion, Casey was woken by a hutia, the small, hairy-tailed rodent found all over Cuba and nearby islands. Like most hutias, this one was an accomplished tree climber, and Casey (himself quite adept at climbing) found himself looking on fascinated at the speed at which this little rodent managed to scale the tallest palm trees. Watching this performance tired Casey out, and after a moment or two, he yawned once more and turned over to continue his siesta.

* * *

Meanwhile, Elina was exploring the Varadero Street market off nearby BelleVue Sunbeach, near Santa Marta. Tee-shirt tops were plentiful, and many of these had been tie-dyed locally into unique patterns. The family was only in the resort for a week, so Elina's needs were just seven day's worth of tops, a couple of pairs of shorts, underwear, a pair of sandals and, of course, swimwear.

Once Elina was set up with her holiday-wear, Maisie suggested they take a look at the souvenirs and leather-goods at the market. Everything they saw was handmade, and they spotted a very attractive leather shoulder bag that Elina thought would be perfect for her on holiday. Her mother spent a moment bargaining with the stallholder, adding a leather belt to the order that she'd have engraved for Tim. Shopping done, they decided to sit for a moment at one of the café bars they'd spotted while browsing the stalls. Elina chose a lemon granizada (very like Slush Puppy), while her mother enjoyed a delicious iced coffee.

Everything complete, they made the next bus back to the resort, and were there in time for lunch in the main buffet restaurant.

Resort buffets are pretty similar wherever you travel. This one was a especially nice one in terms of quality and choice, and eating healthily was a joy rather than a task. Fresh salads and vegetables were expertly prepared and set out, the visual appeal of the whole offering was a sight to behold.

Maisie and Tim were suitably impressed, and in their jobs in the travel company, they were pleased that they'd have a very positive report about the catering facilities on their return home. They sampled a variety of Cuban salads, with innovative mixes of red onion, lime juice, peppers, lettuce, radish, salsa, cumin, avocado, garlic, black bean, mixed greens, almonds, chicory and lots more. Elina also tried several of the salad choices, including one based on watermelon and another with palm hearts. Her favourite, though, was a pasta salad with tuna, basil and rocket, though her father helped her out eating the olives.

Maisie and Tim looked on rather impressed with their daughter's healthy lunch choices. Normally, she would head straight for the fish fingers, nuggets and chips, but here she was filling up on some nutritious and delicious healthy options. Elina looked up and smiled. Her salad selections were all part of a plan!

Buffet restaurants allow eaters to visit the buffet offerings as often as they like, and sometimes, you'll see a person visit several times during a meal. Elina appeared to be particularly interested in the lunch on that Monday, and anyone looking very closely might have noticed that she'd occasionally pop something into her new leather bag. It gradually filled with slices of watermelon, apples, cooked chicken and almonds, so that, by the time their meal was over, her new bag was full to bursting.

Following lunch, the family decided to check out the pool. Tim headed straight to the pool to get two sunbeds next to each other before attending the 1p.m. Welcome meeting, while Maisie and Elina went back to the bungalow to change. As soon as she was alone in her room for a moment, Elina quickly opened the patio doors, crept onto the terrace, parted the branches of the bushes that were hiding Casey and his suitcase, and carefully emptied the contents of her bag for the little fox. Casey opened his eyes, saw the little girl with her stash of delicious looking food, and as their eyes met for a moment, Elina was sure that Casey's eyes said "thank you".

She didn't have time to dawdle, though, so quickly, she stepped back into her bedroom, closed the patio doors and changed into her swimming gear. Then Elina and her mother left the bungalow for their afternoon at the pool.

* * *

Casey had never been so lucky: he hadn't needed to look for food, the small girl had brought enough for at least two days. It was so hot during the day though...

He ate the chicken, which was delicious, and the nuts. He'd eat the fruit later, but first (yawn) perhaps he'd have a snooze.

And so it was: the next Casey know was being disturbed by Elina leaving some more food by his suitcase. As he awoke to the sound and smells, he registered that it was dark, cooler and there was little sound coming from the pool area. Casey made a little sound not unlike a cat's purr, and this was Casey's way of saying thank you to Elina for the food. Elina smiled, and almost put her hand out to stroke the little fox, before reminding herself that foxes are really wild animals, not domestic pets, and could bite.

Instead, Elina smiled once more and whispered "night-night" to Casey, as she slipped away back into her bedroom and closed the patio doors behind her. On his own again, Casey gorged himself on the food he'd been left, before stretching his legs, yawning once more and leaving the safety of his case for another nocturnal adventure.

* * *

Dear reader, do you find you tend to do the same things at the same time most days? Well, lots of us do, and that's partly because routine gives us a feeling of security.

Animals like routine as well, and Casey liked to do things at particular times of the day or night. In the cool of the morning and evening, when it was quieter in the resort, he soon got into the habit of exploring his new territory. He also got into the habit of being around his little suitcase at times when the young girl brought food for him. He was starting to find her presence reassuring. During the heat of the day, though, Casey would sleep, but at night, after everyone had gone to sleep and the noise from humans had muted, that was his time to leave the safety of the undergrowth and really explore.

The hours turned into days, and very soon, Casey found he was feeling very relaxed, living in this new environment, seemingly without predators or pesky border collies. Perhaps this is a place in which he could make a new home. Yes, he'd miss playing with friends like Spike, but he thought he could make new friends, maybe with one of the many hutias he had come across. And there were plenty of balls lying around that they could play with. After five days, Casey was starting to forget the woodland and his vantage point in the trees.

Chapter 12

Casey had never felt so ill...

The day had started as normal: a pre-dawn look around the whole resort, a forage around some of the lush vegetation, a short snooze, then gorging on the fruit that Elina brought back from breakfast, then...

Then the sting.

The scorpions and tarantulas in Cuba will leave a mark but they don't have the venom to kill a human being. In fact, humans are very unlikely to come across either, unless they go looking especially for them. Smaller creatures, though, can be at high risk of serious illness, or worse.

Of course, if Casey had been a local fox, he would have known to avoid the scorpion and give it a very wide berth. Casey, though, would never have come across anything like it and was simply transfixed by its movements in the undergrowth. It seemed to emerge from beneath the soil, then quickly move around the undergrowth, backwards and forwards. Casey watched, captivated, for a while and, though the scorpion didn't come close to him, he wondered if it might make a nice snack.

Up to then, Casey's adventure in Cuba had been quite relaxing. He quickly learned where the resort kitchens were, and occasionally browsed through the rows of bins left outside, full of uneaten buffet food. Of course, he avoided the busy periods in the day, when holidaymakers were out in large numbers – that's the time when foxes usually sleep anyway – and used the cooler parts of the evenings and early mornings to explore the area. The smells and tastes of the resort were all new and exciting to the small fox, and even the chirping sounds that the male crickets made were both new and somehow relaxing to Casey. He'd watch them, fascinated, as they chirped, by either rubbing their long hind legs on their wings or simply rubbing their wings together. The ribbing on the wings intensified this sound, and the warm evening temperatures made their movement faster and therefore more chirping.

He saw Elina regularly, at set times during the day. She'd leave biscuits, fruit and pieces of chicken near his suitcase, he'd look up and (she was sure) smile to say thank you. Then later on, he'd snack, snooze and wait for Elina to arrive later on, after dinner, with some more delicacies.

Through the evenings and into the nights were the times when Casey would stretch his legs, wander around the, by now deserted, resort, explore some of the exotic gardens and plants and observe the wildlife, some very strange to Casey, that lived in the resort.

Crickets, of course, were plentiful. And the males announced where they were by their chirping. They made nice snacks, and so Casey started to feel more confident trying some of these unusual insects and plants.

Until the scorpion...

It was just so interesting to watch. It had eight legs and a pair of grasping pedipalps, which resembled pinchers, and a narrow, segmented tail that it carried in a forward curve over its back. It moved around in jerky movements, a little like a dance, and Casey was mesmerised. He wanted to take a closer look, and maybe even a little snack of the strange insect, so he crept forward, very quietly. The scorpion didn't seem to notice, but just seemed to jump from side to side in this strange dancing motion. Casey took another quiet step forward. Then another. Just one more, and...

...and the scorpion struck!

The tail carried the stinger, and the scorpion brought it down quickly and hard on the little fox's paw, who yelped in pain. The pain was immediate and intense: it grew and became stronger, and Casey tried to make it go away by holding his paw as tightly to his little body as he could. The pain – it was actually getting worse, with a tingling and numbness around the sting. He felt the start of swelling around the sting on his paw and, by now, the pain was almost blinding.

Normally, if threatened, Casey would head back to the relative safety of his suitcase, but the pain from the scorpion sting was so intense, and by now, he was also having difficulty breathing, he didn't make it that far. He did manage to drag himself back into the undergrowth near his little suitcase, with his little heart thumping, then he was very sick indeed.

And that's where Elina found him.

* * *

Some hours later, Elina had been picked up from the Niños Pequeños Club by her mother, Maisie, and they'd joined pa Tim for dinner at one of the speciality restaurants. This was their last evening in the resort, as they'd be leaving in the morning. Maisie and Tim had completed their travel company work, so it was time to head home. This dinner, then, was a small celebration of an enjoyable week spent in this lovely resort.

Elina had mixed feelings. She'd had a lovely time, the Niños pequeños Club was great and she'd made lots of friends, some of whom she would keep in touch with through Facebook. Her best new friend, though, wasn't on Facebook. In fact, her best new friend wasn't a person at all, it was a little fox she'd grown very fond of over the last week. Still, she thought, he seems happy in his new home and will be able to find plenty of things to eat. He didn't really need the treats Elina had brought him anyway. He'd be fine, wouldn't he?

Elina made sure to pop a few special things in her new

leather bag before leaving the restaurant, as a special treat for Casey. A handful of nuts, an apple and some strawberries. The family headed back to their bungalow and kissed goodnight – tomorrow was going to be a long day and they needed an early night.

Elina heard the usual bathroom noises from the en-suite, then the click of the bedroom lights as her parents settled down for the night. That was her signal to quietly open her patio doors and leave her fox-treats out for Casey.

At first, she thought he might have been out in the resort: he wasn't in his usual place in his case. Then she saw him, shaking like a leaf and twitching, curled up in a ball, clearly in pain. She let out a little gasp and dropped the fruit. Instinct kicked in, and without a thought for her own safety, Elina scooped the little fox up into her arms and cradled him gently. Casey looked up and once again, their eyes met, that gentle, knowing look that said "we are friends and will not harm".

It wasn't that late, though quite dark, and of course, Elina didn't want to make any noise that might wake her parents. Thinking quickly, she ran into her bedroom's en-suite bathroom and picked the largest bath towel she could find. Out on the patio, she laid the towel down like a blanket, then wrapped the little fox into the towel to give it some feeling of safety and security. The little fox hardly moved, except to give a sad look to Elina.

There was nothing else Elina could do, other than place a bowl of water next to Casey. But in that moment, Elina had made a decision: somehow, she was going to get the little fox back home to his own territory. All she had to do was figure out how she was going to do that. And in a few short hours, they'd be heading home!

Chapter 13

Elina woke to the sound of a low whimper. She looked at the digital clock on the bedside table: 1:30am. She offered the little fox a few drops of water, and nodded in satisfaction as Casey took them slowly, then licked his lips. She tucked him further into the towel she was using as a warm blanket, and they both slipped back into a broken, disturbed slumber.

By 4:30am, Elina had noticed that Casey's breathing had become a little stronger, and his gaze wasn't quite as weak when he opened his eyes. She had continued, through the night, to hydrate the little fox and made sure he was as cosy as she could make him. That's the best the small child knew. Through the night, though, Elina was sure that the fox had snuggled into her a little more, and his face was reflecting appreciation and (she believed) friendship. Had she understood scorpion stings, she would have been reassured that, in fact, she was doing exactly the right thing under the circumstances, and this was becoming clearer through the night as Casey was showing signs of recovery.

It was also around 4:30am that Elina has concocted her plan to help the little fox get home. She has assumed that the fox's home was near the airport they had flown from, so her aim was to get him back to that airport without anyone finding him. She knew where his old suitcase was, and wondered if it would fit neatly inside the new, larger case that her mother had bought for her a week ago in the Varadero market. She quietly opened the patio doors of her bedroom and retrieved the old case from the undergrowth. It was not at all clean, so she did her best with a towel from the bathroom and cleaned the outside as much as possible. She then got her new case open on the floor, and found the Casey's old case fitted neatly inside, with room to spare for Elina's clothes and other possessions. Good! All she had to do, then, was put enough food inside Casey's case, then tuck the fox inside and her plan would be ready to test!

BREATHING! She realised that Casey would suffocate packed away inside her new case: she would have to make a few air-holes to allow him to breath during the flight home. Luckily, she had a small pair of scissors in her washbag, and these were perfect for fashioning some rudimentary holes in the base of her new case, out of sight from all but the most prying eye. All she would need to do is get plenty of fruit and nuts from the breakfast buffet. Oh, and hope her plan worked...

Just then, Elina heard the alarm clock in her parents' bedroom. 5am, for the early start back to the airport. For this plan to work, then, Elina would need to start right now! She took a deep breath...

* * *

So, the first part of her plan had worked. Elina's parents were delighted that she had packed all her own stuff into her new suitcase and it (and she) was ready for the journey home. That gave them a little extra time to pause at the restaurant buffet. Although the restaurant wasn't open yet (5:30am), the staff had laid out lots of bread rolls, ham, cheese, fruit and cold drinks. They'd also switched on the hot drinks machine so they could take a hot one "to go". Elina stuffed as many pieces of fruit into her new leather bag as it would hold, grabbed a few cans of Fanta orange for herself. Though she'd rather longed for a can of Coke, she hadn't had one in the week they'd been in Cuba. Coke was actually banned in Cuba from 1962 due to political arguments, so Fanta had become a popular alternative drink, especially for tourists. Of course, Cuba had their own local version of cola, but for a nine-year-old used to Coke, it hadn't seemed the same.

Following the grab and go breakfast, the family stopped by the bungalow one last time just to pick up their luggage and say goodbye to the place. Elina took that as an opportunity to pack Casey's little case into hers, along with all the fruit from her bag. She just had time to catch Casey's eyes, and in that instant, she saw a look that said "I'm scared, but I trust you". Elina gave him a little stroke to comfort him, then closed the lid, popped the small case into hers, and zipped it up just as her father came into her room. "All done?" he asked. "Oh yes", smiled Elina, holding onto the handle of her case with one hand, the other hand, with fingers crossed, hidden behind her back.

The journey back to the airport went without drama. It was early morning, and very little traffic on the road, until they were quite close to Havana and the airport. Still, they had plenty of time, and because both Tim and Maisie worked for the travel company, they knew they'd have no problem getting through the Departures area.

Parking right outside the departures entrance, the driver gave a smile and wished the family a happy and safe trip. With all the luggage out of the boot of the car, Elina and her parents wheeled their bags through the main concourse and into the check-in queue. The majority of passengers hadn't arrived at the airport yet, so within a moment or two, they were presenting their tickets at the check-in counter.

The return flight was half-empty. Many of the passengers who had been on the outbound journey with them had decided to extend their holidays for three or even seven days, so this flight was very much below capacity. Maisie presented the family's tickets and passports, and in doing so, the gentleman checking them in must have noticed her identity badge showing she worked for the company. He smiled, typed something into his computer and a moment later, with a flourish, handed Maisie boarding passes for the Business Class area.

No-one can guarantee an upgrade to Business Class, but no-one cannot feel at least a little excited to get one. The check-in clerk gave Maisie a broad Cuban smile, and asked what she would like to do with the baggage. Flying Business Class had given them new options on their luggage. Normally, they would have needed to check them into the luggage hold, but Business Class came with privileges including more hand luggage allowances. Maisie and Tim discussed their options for a moment: given they'd not be arriving home until very late that evening, if they took all their bags onto the aeroplane as hand luggage, it could save them time when they arrived home. Thanking the clerk, Maisie confirmed that's what they'd do.

The clerk nodded his agreement, wished her and her family a great trip home and to see them again soon. "¡Que tengas buen viaje! ¡Nos vemos pronto!" he said, and waved them as they walked away, the whole family delighted at their check-in outcome.

As the family got closer to the Security area, Elina's heart stopped. How would she get the little fox through security without it being spotted by the scanner? She thought about taking Casey's case out of hers in a quiet place and maybe...? No, whatever she did, it felt as if Casey would be discovered and her plan would fail. Oh how she had let the little fox down.

Tim, her father, suddenly grabbed Elina's bag and popped it on the Security conveyer belt. "Gosh", he said, "that's heavier than I expected" he commented with a curious smile. Elina gave a weak smile, but inside, she was agonising that, in the next minute, this whole rescue mission would be over, and she would also be in big trouble.

There were a few bags on the conveyor in front of hers. Her parents' bags, of course, and just one or two more. One by one, she saw each disappear into the scanning machine, re-emerging a moment or so later. As each one went through, Elina's plan would be one step closer to being foiled. By now, she was distraught.

The bag before Elina's father's went into the scanner. A moment later, Elina could see that conversations were happening at the scanning machine, and the operator was pointing to something on-screen. He must have pressed a button, because when the case came out of the machine, it was routed down a different conveyor belt, where a Security agent stood, ready to open and examine the bag and its contents.

All this time, Elina and her parents had been waiting to be called through the people scanner, and now the agent managing this called them forward. Maisie was the first to go, and went through the archway without incident. Next, Elina was called to join her. When she tried to move, though, she was so distressed, she could hardly put one foot in front of the other. "Come on, hunny", encouraged her father, "We don't want to miss the plane!".

Summoning all the courage she could, Elina managed to step through the Security archway, and just as she did, she spotted her case entering the scanner. In a second, her secret would be discovered. Elina could hardly bear it.

Elina and her parents were all through the security archway, and they turned to wait for their cases. Maisie and Tim could see theirs moving down the conveyor belt. Elina's was still in the scanning machine, and Elina could see the operator squinting at the screen. He looked up, and his eyes met Elina's, whose look must have said "please, don't say anything". The operator, though, again examined what was on his screen, and turned around to click his fingers for his supervisor to take a look. Just then, though, there was a huge crashing sound in the Security area, and everyone turned around to see what it was. A tired tourist, looking less than fully awake despite the Hawaiian tee-shirt and colourful shorts, had dropped a whole box of Havana rum onto the tiled floor of the security area. Suddenly, there was glass and rum everywhere, and chaos ensued, with Security people summoning cleaners, re-queuing passengers and re-arranging the conveyor belts to avoid the spillage.

Elina looked back. There was her suitcase, on the conveyor belt, right in front of her. Somehow, in the confusion caused by the rum spillage, the Security agent must have pressed the button to release her bag. She let out a sigh of relief. She couldn't believe her luck. Could her plan still work?

Business Class travel meant that Elina and the family were able to take advantage of the exclusive facilities available to the more wealthy travellers. Terminal 3 is the home of the super-exclusive Salon VIP Lounge. This lounge isn't exclusive based on its amenities, more because most passengers travel in the Economy seats so do not qualify to enter unless they pay an additional fee. Arriving at the entrance to the lounge, Maisie presented their boarding cards to the check-in assistant, who welcomed them into the area and gave them a quick synopsis of what was available, in terms of food, drink, magazines and TV. Probably the best feature of the space, certainly for Elina that morning, was a large window overlooking the crowded departure area below, allowing her to simultaneously observe the chaos and feel grateful to be away from it. Elina could see the episode with the tourist and rum playing out, with the tourist's family now involved in what looked like a huge argument with Security staff, while the conveyor attendant was still looking a little bemused at something. Elina was so pleased the distraction had allowed her to get through with the little fox, unnoticed. Once they all settled into the lounge, though, they were very grateful for the more comfortable upholstered seating and free refreshments, so they did feel slightly privileged while they sat and waited for their flight.

They didn't have long to wait. The priority passengers are always invited to board the flight first, and the Business Class passengers, including Elina and her parents, were therefore some of the first people to board the plane. "Turning left" at the door of an aeroplane is always something that gives a happy experience to a traveller, and this is always enhanced when they see the welcoming faces of the Business Class cabin crew, who always make a special effort with these premium passengers.

On this day, a lady and gentleman guided them to their seats, which were big, luxurious, comfortable and could turn into a bed at the press of a button, if the family wanted to sleep. They had huge screens with which to view movies, TV programmes and music videos, play computer games or listen to audio playlists. Above them were the luggage holds, and again, Tim grabbed Elina's bag and lifted it up into the overhead luggage compartment. He gave a comedy groan as he lifted the case, exclaiming again to Elina "You must have brought the whole bedroom home with you!" as he placed it safely into the hold. This time, Elina's smile back was less troubled and she even managed an embarrassed laugh.

Almost as soon as they had sat down, a cabin attendant was around them offering hot cloths with which to freshen up, and a glass of refreshing juice. As it was relatively early in the day, the champagne would be saved for later. They savoured the juice, and the hot drink that was offered with it, and took the breakfast menu to peruse. Of course, all had eaten at the resort, though some four hours earlier, so they were ready for something now. Maisie and Tim chose fruit, nuts and yoghurt, with a hot bacon roll. Elina chose the honey and nut bar along with a small cheese omelette. Their choices made, the cabin attendant gave a true "Business Class" smile and wished them a happy and restful flight.

Alone again, each of them started to experiment with the various buttons that made their chair first recline, then turn completely flat. Maisie and Tim had flown Business Class before, but this was Elina's first experience, so she was having great fun! Cushions, blankets, soft slippers and ("what's this, Mom – oh, a washing bag!") all sorts of little extras that she'd never had on a flight before. This was going to be memorable.

The family was brought to attention by the tannoy announcement that the aeroplane would be leaving the stand shortly and that passengers were to buckle up. So they put their chairs back upright, put their seat belts on and secured their tray tables, just in time for the safety demonstration which, on this flight, was being presented as a video on their huge screens. They watched the demonstration in silence and prepared for their journey home to begin.

Chapter 14

Casey had slept for most of the night. When he awoke, it was to the reassuring warmth of the towel that was wrapped around him, and the coolness of the water that the little girl gave him. He felt ill, and was still shivering a little, but he did feel a little better than before.

A little later, he felt movement, as Elina placed fruits and berries into his little case, cradled him for a moment, then placed him and the case carefully in a dark, sweet-smelling place. Then again he felt movement as the cases were dragged from the bungalow, first to the resort Reception, then to a car. As the car started its journey, the movement helped rock the little fox to sleep.

Casey had no idea of the passage of time. There were a number of sudden movements that woke him, and he could hear people making noises around him. Then more noises, this time mechanical, then silence. Casey slept.

Later again, Casey awoke to movement, then a sudden lift, then quiet. He had no idea where he could be, but somehow, he didn't feel frightened. He slept.

New sounds woke him again. These were familiar, yet somehow different. First, a shrill, prolonged whining sound, but this sounded quite far away. Next a judder of movement, followed by a weird barking sound, though again this seemed to be more distant than he remembered. Enough, though, to suggest that he was again on an aeroplane, but where he was heading and how long this would take, he had no idea. What he did know, though, was that the aeroplane was moving, and the feeling of movement got more and more distinct, until he felt that strange feeling in his tummy as the flight took off. For an instant, he felt heavier, as he was pushed down tightly into his little suitcase, then after a few moments, that sensation changed again as the aeroplane finished its initial climb and settled to cruise. Next was another familiar whirring sound, familiar, yet again quieter as if coming from a distance.

The fresh smells of the fruit packed around him made him feel a little better, as the poisons from the scorpion's sting were leaving his body. He didn't yet feel like eating, and somehow, the low humming noises around him made him feel sleepy again. He yawned, and slept.

The flight back from Cuba to the UK is often quicker than the outbound journey. The flight out had taken 10 hours, the flight back less than 9, due in part to the wind blowing in the direction of travel. So with the flight leaving Havana airport a little after 9:30am, and given the time difference (Cuba is 5 hours behind the UK) it was 11:30pm as the flight was completing its descent into the homebound airport, and Casey was awoken suddenly by the A330's signature "Bang From the Belly", when a flap under the wing opens and the landing gear drops – usually at around 2,000 feet above the ground.

Moments later, Casey felt a sudden "thump" and a bounce as the aeroplane landed, then a number of distant noises, including a screech (the brakes, with a sensation of speed reduction that brought Casey fully awake), the weird barking sound of the hydraulics, the systems that helps steering, braking, and air pressure, and, once Casey's sensation of movement had finished, that prolonged shrill whine of the electric hydraulic pump used to open and close the cargo doors. This just left the low "hum" of the aircraft, with its soporific effect that made Casey start to doze again. Until...

Sudden movement, as he and the case were jerked out of somewhere and turned over onto their wheels. Then more movement as he (inside the case) felt the case move around on its wheels, first along the straight of the aeroplane isle, then bouncing down steps, then the sounds changing to those of wheels on concrete. Finally, the sounds changed again to clattering up steps, moving along softer ground, and all the time with the sound of people around him. By then, Casey was fully awake, and on edge. Strangely, though, there were familiar sensations as well, including very familiar smells around him. Could he be close to home?

* * *

Maisie and Tim were so happy they'd been upgraded to Business Class. They'd eaten well, and, with the comfort of their special seats, been able to relax and even get some sleep during the long flight. Elina had watched a couple of movies, played a game then drifted off to sleep, so she was more awake than if she'd been in the Economy Class seats.

That said, it was still very later at night, so they were grateful that their upgrades meant they did not have a long wait in the airport while their cases were off-loaded from the aeroplane. They had all their luggage as carry-on, so they had everything with them.

The family didn't live far from the airport – a happy choice, given both Maisie and Tim were regular flyers, as part of their travel company jobs – but as it was so late, Maisie had arranged for the family to stay over at her parent's farm, just a mile or so from the airport. Their car had been left there while they were away, so tomorrow, after a good sleep and hearty breakfast, they'd make their onward journey home a relaxing one.

Tonight, though, they just needed to get through Passport Control and Customs.

Passport Control was easy and quick. Because of their flight upgrade, they were among the first passengers off the aeroplane, and therefore right at the front of the queue, once they'd walked the length of the airport, navigated the several staircases and followed the maze of signs that seem to be common to every airport in the world. Next was Customs.

Elina started to feel distressed again. What if they were stopped in Customs and made to open their cases for inspection? They'd see the beaten up old case with the little fox, and Elina's scheme would be over. They'd call the Police. Her parents would be mad at her. She'd be in huge trouble, and what would they do to the poor fox?

Elina realised there was nothing she could do, except cross her fingers and hope.

The queue for Customs was short, partly because this was the last flight of the evening and partly because they were some of the first people through Passport Control.

Dragging their cases behind them, they walked towards the Customs hall, choosing the green "Nothing to declare" channel. Maisie and Tim had been working mainly, so hadn't really had a chance to do any special shopping, so there was nothing in their cases, they knew, that would attract any import duty. Although Elina had new clothes and suitcase, her parents assumed there would be nothing in her case that would attract attention or incur changes either. So they entered the green "Nothing to declare" channel with the true look of travellers with no guilty secret, though they did look travel-weary.

Customs officers are well-trained to spot people attempting to smuggle goods into the country. Some travellers, hoping to smuggle goods into the country, try to gamble the odds, hoping customs agents don't search their bags or don't find the illegal goods if they do. Experienced agents have seen it all: contraband hidden in shampoo bottles, mobile phones, musical instruments, mini-speakers, just about anywhere. Customs officials can't stop this activity entirely, but they can catch enough of the smugglers to deter others. To stop smugglers, agents rely on a combination of their own experience and sophisticated equipment, including, in some airports, room-sized X-ray machines calibrated to look through a person's clothes for anything suspicious.

On this night, though, they could sense that Maisie and Tim were not attempting to bring in anything they shouldn't. They did look twice at Elina, who did have a strange, pained, guilty look on her face, but as it was past midnight, and Elina was a small girl, they put it down to the long day and journey she'd had, and let her through without challenge.

Once through all the official arrivals stations, they arrived in the main Arrivals hall, and made straight for the Exit. As it was so late, they'd decided to take a taxi from the airport the short distance to Maisie's parents' farm, so they made for the taxi rank just outside the Arrivals hall.

Though it was late, there were a few white taxicabs parked up at the rank, so Tim tapped the window of the first one in the queue, and the driver got out immediately, opening the boot and helped them pop their suitcases in. He turned to the family to smile, and caught a glimpse of Maisie, whom he instantly recognised.

"Maisie, is that you?" he asked. Maisie looked slightly taken aback, then the taxi driver's face registered, and she recognised him as Danny, a school chum from when she lived on the farm as a child.

They spoke for a moment, then the driver realised the family was tired and needed to get on. "Where are you headed this evening?" he asked. "We are staying with Mam and Dad tonight", Maisie said, "so can you pop us over to the farm please? Our car is there and we'll go home properly tomorrow. It's late now and Elina here needs her sleep".

The next moment they were heading out of the airport. The

journey was a short one, just passed all the terminal buildings and offices, past the main car parks, onto the roundabout in the main road, then they turned left down a single track road. Maisie remembered every bump in this road, it was so familiar to her, and within a few moments, they arrived at the gated entrance to her parents' farm, just as she remembered it. Tim jumped out of the car to open the gates, just as a gust of wind made the sign above the gate squeak and it rocked backwards and forwards gently in the breeze. Maisie had heard it too, and the sound was again so familiar to her, as were the faded letters that said "Welcome to Wuxter Farm".

Chapter 15

Bill and Flo Wuxter had been looking forward to seeing their daughter, son-in-law and granddaughter all day. While the old farmer had been out in the fields, Flo had been busy making sure the farmhouse was spick and span in readiness for their visit, and airing the cottage extension, which they had used in the past for holiday rental. This had two ground-floor bedrooms and was, in effect, a self-contained mini-house, with its own small kitchen, bathroom and living room. Flo had thought that the cottage option might be better for Maisie and the family, as they would be arriving so late at night, and would be less likely to be disturbed by the early morning farming activities the next morning.

Incidentally, though Flo and the family used the term "spick and span" for lots of things, the term is more to do with sailing than farming. In the 1500s, a sailing ship was considered spick and span when every spick (nail) and span (wooden chip) was brand-new. On this particular day, though, Flo had made sure that everything in the little cottage extension was perfect, with new bedding, towels and scented candles. The squeaky front and back doors had been fixed, and Flo had insisted that Bill screwed down the window shutters so they didn't flap in the breeze. She was determined they would not be disturbed, and would get a good night's rest when they arrived.

And arrive they did! Though it was very late, it was a little earlier than the Wuxters had expected. The quick entry through the airport had helped, along with the speedy booking of the taxi. Danny, the taxi driver, had known the way to the farm, and navigated the winding track like a rally driver. Withing minutes, they were drawing up to the main farmhouse, and the security lights bathed the car in brilliant white light. Maisie and Tim thanked Danny for the ride, adding a nice tip to the fare, and retrieved their luggage from the boot. By the time they'd done this, Flo had thrown the farmhouse front door open and had her arms open wide in welcome.

Elina was sleepy. Sometimes, even the best behaved children become a little grumpy when overtired, and after the early start, long trip and disturbed sleep en route, Elina was not feeling her best. She'd managed to open an eye and give a weak smile to her Granny, but all she really wanted to do was cosy up into a nice cosy bed and sleep the night away.

Suddenly, from behind Flo, there was a flash of black and white, and Whistle, the old border collie, was out, tail wagging, to welcome the group. Now Maisie had grown from a child to a young lady when Whistle was a young puppy, so he ran up to her first to welcome her home. Maisie stooped to give the old dog some love and attention, and Whistle, excitable as always, did his trademark "round-up" routine, running in circles around Maisie's legs, until...

Whistle suddenly stopped dead in his tracks. And sniffed. And sniffed again. Something had taken his attention away from welcoming Maisie and her family home.

By this time, Bill Wuxter, the old farmer, had appeared, yawning, in the doorway. "What's up, Whistle?" he asked? Whistle, by now, was sniffing around the pathway from the farm towards where the taxi had stopped, and, on the way, paying a little attention to Tim and Elina. Elina... Elina had always loved Whistle, as the old dog had been one of her best friends at the farm on their many visits. She patted the old dog, still tired, but becoming a little more wary, as Whistle began paying close attention to Elina's suitcase. What if the little fox were discovered now, after all the trouble they'd gone through to hide him? She couldn't let that happen.

By now, Elina had fully woken, and her brain was whirring. How to get the dog's attention away from that suitcase?

She remembered her new little leather bag. There might still be something in there that could distract...

She rummaged. She found an orange. Some chocolate. Nothing yet that dogs would eat (or should eat). Then she found a hard-boiled egg she'd taken from the breakfast buffet at the Cuban resort. Now dogs do like eggs. She offered the egg to Whistle, who wagged his tail and accepted the bribe happily. At this, Farmer Wuxter smiled at Elina: "You're spoiled that dog, young lady, and it's time he got some sleep, so he's ready for his morning rounds. Come here, boy" he called the dog, who, very obediently, jumped to his side, though with curious eyes still on Elina's suitcase.

* * *

Whistle was fully awake, and knew something was amiss. That case had a familiar smell - not just the smell of travel, aeroplanes and exotic foreign gardens, but the smell of a fox! And not just any fox: Whistle recognised this was his nemesis, that pesky fox that had been stealing the chickens' eggs and getting away from him, time and time again. He was in that case, and at least, at Whistle's mercy.

"But wait: the little girl is part of my master's family, and was clearly trying to protect the suitcase. Why would she do that? Was that naughty little fox important, in some way, to her? Surely not…

Look! She's brought me an egg! Oh, and my master is calling. I'd better go to him now!

* * *

Casey was holding his breath: he dare not move even a muscle. He was sure that Whistle had found him and was about to give him up to the farmer. The little girl couldn't save him now.

"Please don't give me up" he prayed. *"I'll stop taking the eggs if you let me go"* he promised silently.

He could hear Whistle's sniffing, he could smell Whistle's scent. Any second now, he would be caught and, trapped in the case, there was no escape.

Different noises, the voice of the little girl, then the farmer, and the sniffing stopped. In the suitcase, Casey could hear the dog moving away, then nuzzling up to the old farmer. Could he possibly have escaped capture once again?

* * *

Elina breathed a sigh of relief, but a cautious one: she'd need to help the little fox escape from the farm during the night, or there'd be trouble in the morning. Time to play "tired". Elina feigned tiredness, and her parents understood: time for bed! They thanked Flo and Bill for making the cottage ready, they'd see them in the morning for a mid-morning breakfast, but now, it was time to get Elina to bed.

The cottage was a little way down the path, but the lights were on and everyone knew the way from previous visits. As they made their way, Whistle started following the group, paying particular attention again to Elina and her luggage. Elina attempted to zig-zag along the path to dissuade the old dog from following, but instead, this seemed to encourage his attention. The dog would not leave Elina's suitcase alone.

An elderly voice called from behind: "Come on Whistle, time for bed. Leave them alone now, you can see them in the morning after your morning rounds. Come on boy" and this was followed by a low whistle that turned the old but obedient dog around and a moment later, he'd disappeared through the door to the farmhouse kitchen.

"Whew", thought Elina, as they arrived at the cottage. She

knew she had to help the fox escape, and now she'd realised how little time she had before Whistle was let out in the morning. She needed to act fast!

* * *

Elina made sure that she got the small ground-floor bedroom in the cottage – the one near the back door that led into a small garden that had once been used for growing vegetables. Since the days when her grandparents had used the cottage as a holiday rental, the garden had become overgrown, and so it was that Elina was looking onto that overgrown garden through the bedroom window, waiting for all the lights to go out – both from the cottage and her parents' room and the main farmhouse.

She was fighting tired, and the urge to simply curl up and sleep, but she knew that she only had one chance to let the little fox out of her case before the morning came and it became too late.

The moments felt like hours, and in the quiet of her room, Elina started to hear shuffling sounds coming from her suitcase. The little fox had woken up and was needing to get out.

Casey had recovered somewhat from the scorpion sting and the journey. The sleep had done him good, and also disguised the passing of time, so Casey hadn't felt trapped. Until, of course, the scare a little while ago, when he felt Whistle sniffing around his suitcase.

Trapped in the case, Casey's heart had stopped, his breathing stopped, everything stopped except his fear of being caught by the old farm dog. The sniffing sounds, and proximity of that old dog continued for what seemed to Casey to be ages, but then suddenly, the dog's attention seemed to have moved on elsewhere.

That danger seemed to have passed, and now all was quiet. Casey could sense the little girl was close, and felt the time was right to make it known that he was awake. The only way to do that, he thought, was to move around in the suitcase and make small, subtle sounds. Nothing too obvious, in case Whistle was still close by.

Finally! The last light in the farmhouse had gone out. The cottage garden was in complete darkness, and there wasn't a sound coming from either her parents' room or the farm. Elina needed to act now, or the opportunity would be lost and it would be game over for her and her little friend by the morning.

Moving away from the window, Elina opened her suitcase, pulling the battered old case from within it, gently but firmly by the handle. The shuffling sounds coming from inside the case were louder now, and Elina whispered a "shush", hoping that the little fox would understand. The shuffling noise stopped.

"Good", thought Elina. Moving as quiet as a thought, Elina carried the old case to the bedroom door, then, gently and quietly opened the bedroom door, entering the hallway. A few metres away was the door to the back garden. She turned the torch feature on her smartphone to see better.

"Good", thought Elina again: the key to the back door was in the door lock. She put the case down on the floor briefly, turned the key in the door as quietly as she could, and softly pulled the door open. The cool night air poured into the hallway, and for a moment, Elina worried that the breeze would rattle the doors in the hallway and wake her parents.

Elina held her breath and listened. Nothing. No sounds of

movement from the cottage, nothing from the farm. Whew! She waited another moment, to be sure, but then she started to hear shuffling sounds again coming from the suitcase and she knew she had to finish the job immediately or be found out.

Tenderly, she picked up the suitcase again, taking it into the garden and quietly opening the case fully, so that the two sides of the case were both lying on top of what had been the vegetable patch. She stepped back slightly, a little worried that the fox might leap at her in panic and bite her.

She needn't have worried. After a few long moments, there was another shuffling sound, and from the bundle of old clothes in the battered suitcase, Elina caught a glimpse of two eyes and a long nose. Two tired eyes, blinking in the light of Elina's smartphone torch.

Casey's eyes met Elina's. For a moment, Elina felt she saw recognition, appreciation and friendship in his eyes. Then suddenly, he sprang out of the case and was gone into the night, his longer hind legs giving him the extra spring as he pounced from the crouching position in the case. Elina strained to hear any sound that would give a clue to his whereabouts and waved her smartphone torch around to see if she could see him. Nothing. He'd disappeared as if he'd never been there.

Oh well! Elina did feel a little deflated, but her plan had worked, she had managed to get the fox back home (she assumed this was his home, as he'd come from the local airport originally) and he was safe. Oh, and she'd not been found out either!

She quickly closed the old suitcase and hid it behind the old garden fence. She'd think of getting rid of that in the morning. Now it was bedtime.

With a sigh of relief, Elina quietly locked the back door to the cottage and returned to her bedroom. A moment later, she was fast asleep.

Chapter 16

The next morning, Elina's family woke quite late. Even so, Maisie had to remind Elina several times that it was time to get up. Eventually, though, the smell of fresh sausages coming from the main farmhouse brought Elina to life and, though it was 11:30am, the family were soon tucking into a full English breakfast, with eggs from the farm. In fact, Flo, Elina's grandmother, commented that they were all lucky to have eggs this morning, as an animal, probably a fox, had stolen most of them from the chicken house overnight. At this, Elina felt herself blush very slightly, and did, for a moment, feel a little guilty that, somehow, she was partly to blame for the theft. However, it also meant that the little fox had managed to escape and was fully recovered after its ordeal.

After a very hearty breakfast, the family went back to the cottage to make ready for the onward trip home. This gave Elina the chance she needed to get rid of the old suitcase that had hidden the little fox for so long. She sauntered around the back of the cottage to the old garden and the place she'd hidden the case the night before and...

It was gone!

Elina smiled. The clever little fox must have crept back to the cottage in the night and retrieved the case. He must have had a strong attachment to it, she thought, and now he had it back again, his special place of safety.

So it finally seemed that Elina's adventure was over. Along with her parents, all packed and ready, they spent the afternoon at the farm with the grandparents. Elina loved them both, and understood that beneath the gruffness of Bill, her grandfather, was a loving, caring old man who enjoyed having a little rough and tumble with his granddaughter, out in the fields with the animals. That afternoon, then, was especially interesting to Elina, as while out on the farm, she kept a keen eye open for any sign of the little fox.

Of course, Casey is very shy. He doesn't like to be seen by people, he much prefers to hide amongst the woodland grasses. He was there, though. As Elina stood squinting through the trees near the airport, she was sure the sun reflected briefly on two little eyes perched up in a tree. "Hello little fox", she whispered under her breath, "I wonder if I'll ever see you again"...

* * *

Casey had wanted to put distance between himself and the farm, so as soon as he was released from his old suitcase, he was off, into the night.

Reaching a safe distance, he was able to look back on the farm and, after a while, become a little more comfortable that neither the old farmer nor his dog were around. This, then, was Casey's time, the middle of the night when he felt most at home and he was heartened by the familiar sights, smells and sounds around him. He was home!

Feeling a little more confident, and as he was again in familiar surroundings, he started to think about food. For some reason, eggs came to mind, and, without further delay, and forgetting the promise he'd made to himself just an hour or two before-hand, Casey made his way back towards the farmyard where he knew that bounty from the chickens would be available. As always, though, Casey knew that the best way to grab a few eggs without waking the family was to creep into the chicken coop without frightening them, or taking all the eggs. And that is exactly what he did. He crept through the gap in the fence that only he knew existed, popped the first three eggs into his mouth, to keep them safe, and crept back through the gap.

He was just about to make his way back to the safety of his woodland and his special place of safety, when he realised that his case was still lying open in the cottage garden. He needed to retrieve that, and quickly. He could already see that sky was starting to show signs of morning, which meant that the old farmer, and (more importantly) his dog would be on their rounds soon.

Wasting no time, Casey padded gently around the back of the farm house to the cottage garden. Casey could see the case where it had been earlier when he'd made his escape. Everything was still there and in one piece. Carefully, Casey placed the three eggs within the pile of old clothes and gently closed the case, muffling the "click" with his body. He looked around to check he hadn't been seen, and was relieved that no lights had gone on in the buildings, and no sound was coming from anywhere on the farm. Good, everyone was asleep.

Casey just needed to get his little suitcase back into the woodland and to its home in the undergrowth, and he did this just as gently and silently as he could. The little case, though not very heavy for a person, was not the easiest for a small fox to move, and by the time he got to his special place in the wood, it was becoming much lighter. Time, he thought, to tuck up inside that case, eat one of those eggs and have a snooze. And that is exactly what he did.

* * *

Later that afternoon, Elina joined her grandfather and faithful dog Whistle for a walk across the fields, checking that everything was as it should be. Elina, of course, was very keen to see if her little fox was around, and paid very close attention to any movements in the undergrowth for any signs he might be there. Whistle, of course, know that the cheeky little fox was around – he had caught the scent – and pulled on his lead so that the party moved towards that scent. Maybe today, he'd finally catch the fox, though something had changed: Whistle had noticed a connection between the fox and the little girl, who was clearly trying to protect him last evening. He didn't know why, but he did know that his loyalty extended from the old farmer to his family, and that included the little girl. Maybe he'd give the fox a break today.

Farmer Wuxter left Whistle with Elina for a moment, while he went to feed the chickens.

From his perch in a tree, Casey could see the old farm dog across the field, accompanied by the little girl who had helped him, and he felt a wave of fondness pass through him. She had helped him, fed him and probably saved his life, and brought him home. He didn't know if they'd meet again, of course, but for a brief moment, he felt a connection to the girl as their eyes met one last time. In that moment, he also understand something about Whistle for the first time. The loyal old dog was part of the farmer's family, and so was the little girl. Perhaps he ought to be nicer to him in the future. Perhaps...

As the party started to turn away, Casey gave Whistle a big cheeky wink, and watched with glee as the old dog pulled sharply on his lead.

Somehow, Casey didn't think his adventures were over...

Printed in Great Britain
by Amazon

74981843R00071